Shed Light
on Death

Also by L. A. Taylor

Deadly Objectives
Only Half a Hoax
Footnote to Murder

SHED LIGHT ON DEATH

L. A. Taylor

Walker and Company
New York

First published in the United States of America
in 1985 by the Walker Publishing Company, Inc.

Published simultaneously in Canada by John Wiley & Sons
Canada, Limited, Rexdale, Ontario.

Library of Congress Cataloging in Publication Data

Taylor, Laurie.
  Shed light on death.

  I. Title.
PS3570.A943S46   1985   813'.54   85-10602
ISBN 0-8027-5630-1

Printed in the United States of America

10 9 8 7 6 5 4 3 2 1

Fox Prairie, Minnesota, is an imaginary locale, as are the town it shares a high school with and its county seat. The rest of Minnesota is quite real and may be found in any U.S. atlas. All the characters in this novel and every one of their actions are entirely fictional and are not based on any real persons or incidents.

FIRST

AT THE HEIGHT of the evening rush hour a brilliant light appeared in the sky east of the Twin Cities, moving slowly south along the low, dusty-green hills that separate the St. Croix and the Mississippi. Within minutes, traffic on the interstate between Minneapolis and St. Paul—first eastbound, and then westbound as well—slowed even beyond its usual late-afternoon crawl and finally edged to a stop.

A few drivers got out of their cars and squinted through their sunglasses, hoping for a better look despite the rising waves of heat. When the state patrol officer driving along the shoulder of the road looking for an accident to explain the traffic jam saw the first pair of binoculars trained on the sky, he sighed and abandoned his air conditioning to stand in the traffic fumes beside his own car. A minute later he had spotted the light, and the crackle of his radio alerted the news media as well as his fellow officers. Three TV vans and a helicopter swung out of their intended routes and headed east.

The thing sailed on southward with a bobbing motion that made a few people nod in recognition: this must be what was meant by the "skipping stone" travel of flying saucers. It had no motor anyone could hear. Two hours later, a twin to the first light appeared in the southern sky and shone steadily for an hour or more. No mystery in that. People in the southern sectors of the cities were used to seeing airplanes hanging motionless in the sky—it simply meant that the line of travel of the UFO was precisely aligned with the line of sight of the person watching.

Channel 4's traffic-observation helicopter trained a TV camera on the first bright object, showing it to be rounded, with a pointed base, and glowing with a pinkish-yellow light. The pilot identified it as a huge weather balloon. The avuncular anchorman

1

on the 6:00 P.M. news repeated both the tape and the identification. So did the weatherman. On Channel 5, file pictures of weather balloons were shown, and the weather segment of the news consisted chiefly of a capsule history of the use of balloons in meteorology. At 10:00, the object to the south was identified in an exclusive live interview with a bemused astronomer from the University of Minnesota as the planet Jupiter, now entering a phase of unusual brightness.

Despite all this coverage, phone calls continued to pour into both stations' newsrooms, and into the newsrooms of other local TV and radio stations. Phones at the Minneapolis *Star and Tribune* and the St. Paul *Pioneer Press* rang as they were cradled.

At the Minneapolis paper, one editor pulled the plug on her phone as she spotted one of her reporters passing through the newsroom. "Hey, Jack," she yelled.

Jackson Powell stopped with the suddenness of a man running into a wall and slowly approached the editor's desk. "You know this UFO thing?" she asked. "Get on it. Call up some of the local guys—Cameron Rogers over at the U, and . . . what's the name of that other guy, the one from CATCH?"

"I don't know," Powell said. "I don't follow UFOs."

"Sure you know." The editor prodded his memory with impatient jabs of her pencil. "The guy that got mixed up with that murder a few years ago?"

"Oh, him." Powell tugged at his fair hair to bring the memory out of hiding. No good. "I know who you mean, but I can't think of his name, offhand."

"Well, think of it, and get interviews with both of them. Check out the library. We'll see what we can put together for a full-page analysis. We might get it in Sunday."

Powell rotated his pudgy body on one heel.

"And make it a good one. I'm sick to death of the phone ringing itself blue every time a flock of geese decides to take off at sunset."

"It wasn't geese, it was a balloon," Powell retorted, just to show that he hadn't been hibernating all evening. "And it wasn't at sunset. Ten after five." He took care to toss these comments

2

over his shoulder as he walked away, and he walked away a lot faster than he'd responded to the editor's shout.

She got in the last word, after all: "Try to keep your temper, will you?" she called. "I hear this Rogers can be a number-one bastard."

The piece went together in the quick workmanlike way of newspapers. At the story conference the editors decided to give it a good play, and a staff artist produced a suitably amusing illustration of bleeping little men descending from a weather balloon. Early on the planned Sunday morning, the page, padded in the fat fold of the rest of the newspaper, dropped with a *thuck!* at the doors of hundreds of newsstands and hit the front steps of thousands of houses.

In one such house the page was read with far greater attention than in most. When the coffee reheating on the stove boiled over, the paper lay abandoned, open, on the table where it had been read. One by one the pages caught the cool breeze of the air conditioner beside the table and crawled across the flattened section to the other side, until the newspaper lay completely shut and shivering lightly—perhaps at the strange idea that had just fluttered to life among its gray columns.

I

THE PHONE STARTED ringing at the same moment our elderly neighbor rapped on the glass of our back door. "Could you get that, Joe?" Karen asked as she headed for the door, where Mrs. Eskew had her nose pressed to the glass, peering through the thin curtain.

I stretched backward from my seat at the kitchen table to hook the receiver off the wall phone and muttered some kind of hello without really taking my eyes off the Sunday sports section.

"Hey, J.J.," said a slightly gravelly voice. "It's Ed Gustafson. Remember me?"

"Sure I do," I replied, grinning. I'd only talked to Ed maybe half a dozen times, but he's a nice guy, a UFO enthusiast from a small town maybe forty miles south of Minneapolis, where I live. What I'd talked to him about was mostly flying saucers—I'm a field investigator for an outfit called CATCH, the Committee for Analysis of Tropospheric and Celestial Happenings. UFOs, in other words.

"I got a sighting, right outside town here." The glee in Gustafson's voice would have suited the winner of the grand prize in the Publisher's Clearing House Sweepstakes. "It's got everything you wanted. When can you come down?"

The cool scent of fall air swirled into the kitchen with Mrs. Eskew. I nodded to her and held out my cup for more coffee as Karen started to pour. "Everything I wanted?" I repeated, with a sort of forlorn excitement building somewhere in my lower chest.

"Karen, a board just broke in your back step," I heard Mrs. Eskew say, but Gustafson was talking too.

"Like you and Cameron Rogers said in that newspaper story, remember?" Gustafson reminded me. "Back in August, when

4

you knobheads up in the cities got all in a tizzy over a weather balloon?"

"Oh." Two months before, when both the Twins and the international news had been in a late summer slump, a particularly low, bright weather balloon had drifted southward east of St. Paul, and a lot of people had wondered what it was. A *lot* of people. Most of whom had called radio or TV stations or the newspapers, hoping to satisfy their curiosity. To top that off, Jupiter, after stealthily brightening behind a week-long screen of evening thundershowers, revealed itself on the same clear night, and a lot more people wondered what *that* bright light might be. The city newspapers, both of them, had given fervent thanks and diluted the ads on a couple of pages each with articles about UFOs. The Minneapolis paper had featured interviews with me and with a guy from the university, and the other guy—Cameron Rogers, Ph.D.; I knew him slightly—had talked me into saying in print that I'd help him investigate any case that met certain criteria, all neatly laid down in the article. Now Gustafson was apparently calling in my chips.

"So when can you come?" he demanded. Karen, giving Mrs. Eskew a hand with her sweater, glanced at me as she draped it over the back of a chair. I avoided her eyes.

"Gee, I don't know," I said. "It's a little hard for me to just drop everything—I'd have to do some arranging. When did this happen?"

"Just last night. It's a beaut. I got a guard on the landing site right away."

"*Landing* site?"

Karen's head snapped up. She stared at me. Very slowly, she sat down and picked up her coffee cup, lowered it to the saucer without drinking, and brushed her hand across her forehead. Mrs. Eskew chattered on, oblivious.

"I told you it had everything you and Cam Rogers wanted."

"Have you talked to him, Ed?" I temporized.

"Sure have. He's gonna run down first thing tomorrow morning. So what about you?"

"Well . . . " Somehow, I got off the phone without making any firm commitment, and faced Karen.

"A landing site?" she said, gazing into space. "I hope it's in maybe Montana?"

"Actually, no. It's in Fox Prairie."

"Something landed in Fox Prairie?" Mrs. Eskew bobbed toward me with an eager grin. "Why, my husband's sister used to live there! It's just a little bit of a town, but such a pleasant place." She nodded her blued curls. "I spent many a summer there myself, with the children. We had a little cottage we rented near his sister, on Pintail Lake, and Reuben would come down every weekend." She broke off, and a faint grimace passed over her lined face. "That was before Sarah's husband passed away and she moved back up here. What landed? A flying saucer?"

"The man on the phone thought it might be," I said carefully.

"Think of that!" I hadn't seen Mrs. Eskew so animated since the time she took a shot at somebody trying to break into her house, and then came over and shot out my screen door showing me how she'd done it. "In Fox Prairie, of all places! You'll be going down there to look into it, of course. I'll call Sarah and see who you should talk to." Mrs. Eskew seemed to think this needed explanation: "She's the sort of person who keeps up old friendships, even when she moves away."

"Well . . ." I shrugged an apology at Karen. "Karen and I have an agreement. No investigations more than twenty-five miles from home. And Fox Prairie's more like fifty or fifty-five."

"Oh, is that why you don't go to North Dakota anymore!" Mrs. Eskew exclaimed. "I'd wondered about that."

I've been to North Dakota exactly twice in my life, but I let it pass. The second trip resulted in Karen's and my agreement— Karen's ultimatum, maybe I should say—which I'd had some cause to regret. The worst occasion was in March of '84, when a cop and a sheriff's deputy in Bennet County, South Dakota, had been within two hundred yards of an unexplained array of lights I'd have given my eye teeth and my good right arm just to see. Childish me: I sulked for a week after that one. But then, so did Prue Watson, the head of CATCH, and she's a lot older than I am.

"A landing?" Karen repeated. I couldn't read her face, and her voice was flat. "Who was that on the phone?"

"Ed Gustafson. You remember him."

She ran her fingers through her hair, frowning. "Oh, yeah. That guy who asked you to talk to his club last year. Man in his early sixties, wears a cap, very fit and cheerful? Looks like he was put together out of spare parts?"

"Good spare parts. That's him."

"And he says something landed in Fox Prairie?" Meaning: What's going on? You've never found anything to support the idea that flying saucers are really extraterrestrial, and this Gustafson seemed like a rational man.

"*Something* happened last night that's got him excited," I said. "He's asking me and Cam Rogers to come down and look the thing over. Because of that newspaper story last summer."

"Oh, yes," said Mrs. Eskew. "Because you promised."

"I knew that would be trouble." Karen tightened her lips and stared at the table.

We fell into a silence measured by the shriek of the chains on the backyard swing, where my son and a couple of neighbor kids were playing. Karen began to fiddle with one of her little gold earrings, as if turning it back and forth could unlock something in her mind. Mrs. Eskew looked from one of us to the other and poured herself some more coffee. It smelled good; I reached for the pot and warmed up what was left in my own cup.

"Your back step's broken, J.J.," Mrs. Eskew said.

"I know."

"It really ought to be fixed."

"Thanks. I'll get to it as soon as I can."

Karen screwed her mouth into an exasperated grin and sighed through her nose. "Well, fifty miles," she said. "I guess we'd better make an exception this time." The end of the sentence sounded wistful; she glanced at me, almost shyly. "I wish I could go with you."

I blinked at that. "You haven't gone along on an investigation for six years," I pointed out.

"Because of Joey," she reminded me. "Before that, I went

7

along whenever I could, you know that." She stopped and swirled what was left of the coffee in her cup. "It was kind of fun, wasn't it?"

"Why don't you both go, then?" Mrs. Eskew asked. "You'll love Fox Prairie. It's so lovely in the fall, especially along the creek bottom. Red maple, sumac ... "

"With Joey in school," Karen said to her cup.

"Joey can stay with me." As usual, Mrs. Eskew sounded as if she thought herself the only person capable of solving the problem at hand. "I can see him to the bus in the morning and go down to the corner and meet him at noon. You won't have to worry about a thing. And if he wants to have some of his little friends over, that's just fine with me. Won't do me any harm to get my hand back in at baking cookies."

"Well ... " Karen said.

"And if he wants to play on his swings, that's okay too. I can see them from my kitchen window. And I still have that emergency key to your back door, so he can get anything of his own he wants. Or, I could come to stay over here, if you'd like that better."

"He likes kindergarten," Karen said, convincing herself.

"Oh, yes. He wouldn't want to miss that, not at all," Mrs. Eskew agreed.

For once I had the sense to keep quiet and let her do the talking, and within five minutes she bounced out into the backyard to talk to Joey.

"Are you sure about this, Kay?"

She nodded. "I've been thinking lately. . . . I haven't really been fair. I've got my writing, and you support that. And the UFOs ... well ... it's not that I want you to use up all our vacation time and money driving to North Dakota in a blizzard again"—I winced—"but Fox Prairie's so close, and you haven't had anything to investigate for a couple of years now."

"Almost three and a half." The bleak sound of my own voice surprised me.

"See? I knew you must be missing it. So yes, let's go. It shouldn't take more than a couple of days, should it?" Karen leaned toward me, her face brightening. "It can be a kind of

8

vacation, just the two of us. We haven't done anything like that in years."

"Cameron Rogers would be there," I warned her.

"Cameron Rogers doesn't count."

"You've never met him," I said. "He has a way of making himself count. Remember how I complained about that newspaper thing? That the reporter gave Rogers all the good quotes, even when I was the one who had said them?"

Karen shrugged. "So, I won't talk to reporters." She got up and set her cup in the sink. "You should see my journal," she complained. "Every entry looks like every other one. Even my dreams are all the same. I can't write if I go stale." Suddenly she grasped the edge of the sink and stiffened. "Ed Gustafson didn't say anything about any dead bodies, did he?" she asked.

"Not a word." I'd have laughed, except that I'd actually encountered a couple in the past as a result of my working for CATCH.

"Joe, promise me, if trouble comes up, we'll come straight home?"

"Okay." I was already looking back at the newspaper to see how the Vikings were doing.

"Then that's all right," Karen said.

"Hey, Mom!" The back door whacked against the kitchen counter as Joey hurtled into the house. "Am I really going to stay with Mrs. Eskew for a couple of days?"

"Only if you want to," Karen said.

"Oh, boy! Right away?"

"Maybe starting tomorrow," I said.

"Hey," yelled my one and only child, running out the back door into the yard, "you guys, guess what?"

Kids. Sometimes they have a way of making their parents feel downright superfluous.

II

AT WORK, I'M not superfluous. I'm a unit manager now, instead of a lowly engineer, and it took me most of the next morning to settle things so I could get away, even though my unit had just met one deadline and the next was two months off in a future that has a way of stretching unpredictably in the business my company's in. Cameron Rogers applied his Ph.D. to some kind of biological research over at the university; he had a lab to run and four technicians to be told how to do it, so it was noon and then some before we converged at my house that Monday. The school bus roared away from the corner as I stepped out of my car.

"Hi, Dad!" Joey yelled, running toward me with crayonned papers clutched in both fists. "Di'n't you go yet?"

"Hi!" I staggered back as he tackled me with a hug. "Where's your jacket?"

"Ooh." Brief contrition. "Lef' it at school. Oh, well, I can get it tomorrow," he said, with the confidence kids have in good weather's lasting forever. He ran up to the front door, where Karen was waiting for him, and Rogers rolled to the curb and lifted one hand in greeting.

Rogers drove a red Triumph, a little stingy on room for anything other than two people and an engine, so we'd agreed to take my station wagon and drive down together. The night before I'd run an incredible security gauntlet to pick him up at his brand-new condo so we could stop at his lab to load some of the stuff he seemed to consider indispensible for his own UFO investigations: a scintillation counter (one of the little green men might have spat on the ground as he left and the spit could be radioactive); a magnetometer, in case they'd rucked up the local magnetic field; test tubes containing nutrient soup or dollops of agar so any germs they might have shed could be "grown out," as Rogers put it; the heavy-duty cooler he kept the test tubes in, and a couple of things he didn't bother to explain, impressive gadgets with black leather cases and dials marked off with lots of fine lines and elegant red numerals. I tossed in my own stuff—my notebook; a steel measuring tape; a couple of boxes of Ziploc bags in different sizes, to hold specimens; and CATCH's battered Minolta (the dozen extra rolls of film were in my suitcase) and considered us especially well equipped.

Rogers prowled the sidewalk while I got rid of my necktie suit and Karen and I settled Joey with Mrs. Eskew. "My, what an elegant man!" Mrs. Eskew remarked, glancing out her open front door at Rogers. "You'd better be on your guard, J.J.—or tall-dark-and-handsome out there might sweep Karen away!" The arch little smile that went with the caution pricked a flare of annoyance. I almost called the whole deal off, right there.

She was right, though. Elegant was the word for Rogers. He and I both wore jeans, joggers, and sweaters; the difference was that Rogers looked dressed for an ad for men's cologne in *The New Yorker,* while I (as usual) managed to look like something somebody else's mother would give a dirty look to on her way through the room. How people like Rogers do it, I don't know.

"Quite the homebody, aren't you, Jamison?" he commented, as Karen and I reached the sidewalk. Somehow, coming from him, with the faint upward flick of one eyebrow, it sounded like something I should have kept hidden. I gritted my teeth as I unlocked my car. What kind of "vacation" were Karen and I going to have?

On the porch, Mrs. Eskew made a megaphone of her hands and called, "I'll try Sarah again today."

"Thanks," Karen called back, from the seat behind me. "Bye-bye, Joey! See you soon!" The kid almost waved himself right off the top step as the car drifted past Mrs. Eskew's house.

"Have you talked to Gustafson at any length about this?" I asked, once we were finally pointed south on 35W.

Rogers flicked a glance at Karen, who was riding behind me.

"Not really. I think he wants us to interview his witnesses on our own, take a look at the site without any gift ideas."

"Good idea," Karen said.

Rogers yanked enough play into his seatbelt so he could turn sideways and smile at Karen. "Do you always help your hubby out on his field trips, Kay?" he asked.

I gripped the steering wheel a little harder and heard my back teeth click. Kay is *my* name for Karen. And I couldn't believe I'd used it with Rogers around; it's too close to private.

"Karen," Karen said pleasantly. "No."

Hubby registered too. I took a sudden dislike to Rogers's aftershave, something expensive someone had once given me a drop or two of. I was glad I'd never felt flush enough to buy more.

"You'll enjoy this," Rogers was assuring my wife. "I'm sure you'll find it fascinating to observe a competent investigation. It's lucky that my head technician got back from his hunting trip in time to take over for me at the lab. I'd hate to be late for this one."

"Hunting trip?" My mental image was something more like army field exercises, but then I'm not a hunter.

"It's birdie and bunny season, didn't you know?" Rogers turned easily back to me. "This technician of mine likes to tramp around in the fields taking potshots at birds. Comes back all scratched up, feeling really macho. I got all that out of my system years ago." Rogers paused for a moment and chuckled. "If you'd ever seen his wife, you'd think he could get his macho jollies a lot better by staying home, but him—he even drives something called a 'Sportsman.' "

"He's running your lab while you're gone?" I asked, anxious to deflect the topic.

"Oh, yes. Bucky's not too bad at that," Rogers acknowledged. "He's been with me over ten years now, so he knows most of the routine." He chatted on about the research he was doing, something with vitamins. To me it sounded like so much effort to duplicate somebody else's results, but he seemed to think it required nothing short of genius. And maybe there were some original bits, what do I know?

After a while I stopped listening and looked out at the dark, recently turned fields, where chunks of cornstalk poked out of the ground here and there and flocks of blackbirds scoured the clumped earth for stray kernels. A green sign slowly enlarged at the side of the road, only to zip behind us when we drew even: exit to Northfield, a small town snuggled in the embrace of two famous colleges. Almost twenty miles to go, I calculated, every inch beside this man who gave me the same impression of coiled energy I'd once had while watching timber wolves in Como Park.

Suddenly I realized that he'd shifted subjects and was talking about CATCH. "It's true, isn't it, that it's run by a little old lady in Boston?" he asked.

"Prunella Watson." I grinned, thinking of her. "She's something else."

"Knits afghans, I bet," Rogers remarked. "Knitting, cats, and UFOs. They go together in a certain kind of frustrated old maid."

Prunella Watson, spinster teacher (retired), owned two orange tabby cats, and every Christmas without fail she sent me or Karen or Joey a hand-knit scarf, but I didn't think any of that was Cameron Rogers Phid's business.

Ed Gustafson had directed us to the only motel in Fox Prairie, one of those plain clean places you're sometimes lucky enough to find in the country. A quarter mile out of town we passed the sign for a restaurant Ed had recommended, both as place to eat and as landmark. Already a little hungry, I hoped we'd be able to get back to it sometime before dark. The motel hunched around a small courtyard a couple of hundred yards farther down the road, just as Ed had told me when I'd called him to explain what Rogers and I had arranged for today. We bumped across a strip of rough, poorly repaired road and into the drive, where I parked beside an arrow-shaped sign that said *Office,* got out, and stretched hard before going with Rogers up to the motel's glass door. We played do-si-do with a young man who'd just finished using the pay phone outside the office and got ourselves assigned to rooms.

A dusty green Ford pickup pulled into the courtyard while we were still taking suitcases out of the station wagon, and jerked to a stop so close I jumped. Ed Gustafson climbed down from the cab, looking just as fit and cheerful as Karen had remembered him, the sleeves of his plaid wool shirt rolled back over tanned arms glinting with sparse white hairs, blue eyes clear as a boy's shining through his farmer's squint.

"Hey, how ya doing?" he greeted me. I got a quick, firm handshake and a cuff on the shoulder before he turned to Rogers with the hand outstretched. Rogers took the hand, in no hurry. "And you're Dr. Rogers, right? Ed Gustafson." Karen stepped out of our room and came toward us, smiling.

"Well, hey!" Gustafson hailed her. "Nice to see you. You're looking fat and sassy. How's your boy?"

Karen's put on a little weight since Joey was born, just enough to make it obvious that she was too thin before. Fat, no. She did look good, framed against the dark shingled building, though her jeans were faded in streaks and the cream-colored turtleneck that set off her honey-brown hair already had a smudge on one elbow.

"She does look good," Rogers murmured. I moved away a couple of steps; what sounded like pure good spirits from Gustafson made me want to give Rogers the back of my hand across his mouth. *Good God*, I thought. *What the hell did I get myself into, working with this guy?*

"You want to go straight on out to the landing site?" Gustafson asked. "Or you want to talk to some witnesses, or run down the road for a cup of coffee and let me tell you what I've got?"

"Landing site," Rogers declared. I'd have opted for coffee myself, but Gustafson had already opened the creaking door of his pickup.

"You better follow me out there," he said. "Ain't enough room for four in the cab, and the bed's filthy."

"Oh, will you be coming?" Rogers asked Karen.

She smiled, a kind of smile I hope I never get from her, and yanked open the back door of the station wagon. "Yes," she said, and got in and slammed the door.

It took me a minute, while I closed the room up and searched all my pockets for the car keys, to see why she'd decided to ride in back again. Rogers would probably have made it three across in the front seat, and if we were going to do this investigation together with any semblance of civility, what could she say about it?

Gustafson led us back through town. As Mrs. Eskew had told us, it was small: a prairie town with a two-block-long core of tan and deep maroon brick, single-story buildings topped with the useless crenellations that were in favor at the turn of the century; a farmer's co-op with a blue and white metal sign and a bunch of other stores I didn't take time to identify, some of them empty. A big granite Lutheran church breasted a wave of evergreens that threatened to break over the town's one intersection. At one end of the main street, a gas station guarded the approach; at the other a miniature Red Owl supermarket had been first to greet us. The traffic light didn't slow us down any; Gustafson took a right onto more two-lane blacktop. Fox Prairie ended abruptly after three residential blocks and the green pickup doubled its speed.

I pushed the station wagon up to sixty-five to stay with him, but even so a couple of cars and a van passed us, tooting at Gustafson's truck. He tooted back. Neighbors, probably.

The scenery was much as it had been to the north. A little flatter, maybe, but still composed of fields readied for winter or grazed by cows drooping with boredom. Along the side of the road, bands of brush widened and thinned; sumac flaming, the yellow flags of dogwood, a hundred other plants from weeds to small trees that I couldn't have named even if I'd been traveling slowly enough to make them out. Once a rabbit hopped onto the road ahead of us. After a couple of indecisive zigzags it dashed back into the bushes it had come from. Whether it was better off there was a moot point; two men in blaze-orange jackets had climbed out of a van a quarter mile down the road, carrying long drab gun cases.

About four miles out of Fox Prairie, Gustafson abruptly slowed and turned off the road into a driveway. I stamped on the brakes and fought my barge into the driveway after him.

He'd already stopped and was walking back along the side of the pickup.

"Hey, you know you've got no brake lights?" I called.

He paused and looked back at his truck and pushed his cap up on his head a bit. "That a fact?" he said. "Thanks." He came up to my window and leaned on the edge of the opening. "I'm gonna leave my truck here and come along with you," he said. "You'll have to let me out with fifty yards to go, though, so I can so to speak ring the doorbell, or my guard's likely to pull a shotgun on you."

"Okay," I said. Gustafson circled behind the car and got in next to Karen.

"You'd better go around my pickup and make your turn in the yard," he instructed. "Miller won't mind."

I sure didn't want to back out onto that highway and get my rear end torn off, so I did as Ed said. The farm the driveway led to looked deserted, though a big black dog chained to the barn got to his feet and lifted his ears at us as I turned the station wagon around, and an orange and white cat lolled on one of the back-porch steps with chin and paws draped languidly over the edge. Through my open window wafted a pungent odor I'd last smelled when I followed a truckload of hogs halfway across the state of Wisconsin, though the animals themselves were somewhere out of sight and hearing. We bumped through our circle and down the drive and made the right turn onto the highway.

Less than a quarter mile down the road, Gustafson held up a hand for me to stop and let him out. I got off the pavement onto the shoulder, which seemed pretty solid, and waited until he waved me on.

By the time I'd pulled up and parked the wagon, there were two men waiting. Just as Gustafson had said, the second man carried a shotgun, broken open for safety's sake and slung over his arm with a look of belonging. I remembered that it was small-game season.

"Nobody'll pay much attention to one station wagon alongside the road," Ed said as I got out. "Put the truck there too and we'd have a hundred guys and their dogs stop to see how the hunting was."

16

I nodded and got myself introduced to Herman Miller, a twin to Ed in age and good cheer, on whose land we stood.

"Been keeping folks away, like Ed said," he told us. "Damn near every kid from the high school been out some time or other, seems like. But I ain't let any of them down off the road."

Fortunately for Rogers and me in our soft low shoes, it had been a dry fall. We jumped the grass-filled ditch beside the road and followed Gustafson through some shrubby growth to a three-strand fence of barbed wire to have our first look at the landing site. Sparrows rose at our feet and fluttered away chirping.

"I brought you through this way because of the footprints," Gustafson explained. "There's some little ovals like bootprints that go from the place where the ground's all flat to the bushes. The fence is down there, too—only not cut with cutters. You'll want some pictures."

Pictures. It was a fresh roll of film in the camera, but the rest was back in my suitcase, almost five miles away. I swore silently at myself and resolved to plan my shots so that thirty-six would be enough.

"Here, come on through," Miller said. "Got to put up a new section anyway, and no sense spoiling your nice pants." The glance was for Rogers; nobody in his right mind would worry about the jeans *I* had on. Miller produced a pair of wirecutters. "Stand back, this'll spring," he warned, and cut the top two strands of the fence. "Figured you'd want to take samples," he said. "So I brought along the cutters."

The saucer, if that's what it was, had landed, if that's what it did, near the fence but on the field. The earth of the field had been broken into small clods in places; Miller's bootprints, where he had crossed the field from his house to look at the spot, were clearly visible as lighter patches in the dark soil. A big circular patch was also lighter, simply because the clods of earth had been pulverized and reflected the afternoon sun a little better. The circle was maybe twenty feet across; the closest part of it was about six or seven feet from the fence. I'd get all those measurements for sure later. Just now I wanted a picture, one that would show the three small, sharp, round depressions set in a triangle within the larger circle, with the barn roof and silos in the background to identify the spot.

Small oval prints led from the large circle to a break in the fence. I moved closer and took a picture of those, too, with a longer lens. "Place looks untouched," I commented.

"Told you I'd put a guard on it," Gustafson reminded me, with a touch of justifiable pride.

"I'd better bring my equipment down the same way we came," Rogers said, turning to survey the wide strip of brush and brambles between the road and the fence. "I'll want to know where those footprints go, and why. Is that color or black-and-white you've got, Jamison?"

"Color."

"Too bad. We should be using black and white. It blows up a lot cleaner for the magazines, and it's cheaper to reproduce."

Magazines! Trust Rogers to be thinking that far ahead. "I've got some black-and-white back in my suitcase," I said.

"Good. Once I get my instruments out of your car, your wife can go back and get it." Rogers headed back along the fence without waiting to see whether Karen agreed.

"Real take-charge guy, ain't he?" Miller remarked. "What's this equipment he's talking about?"

"Oh, he's got all kinds of stuff. Measures radioactivity and magnetic fields and God knows what all." I squatted down for a better look across the site. The place where the saucer had landed was virtually flat, a small level area about the size of a city lot from which the ground sloped gently upward toward the west, away from the road, and a little more steeply, as the road did, toward north and south. Standing, you could see Miller's three blue silos, the top of his barn, and a chunk of the green roof of his house among the yellow-leafed elms that surrounded it. No one in a normal position in the farmyard would be able to see into the little level place. "You didn't notice anything out here on Saturday night?" I asked.

"Nup. First I knew was Ed here calling me up, and by that time the thing was gone."

"You came down in the dark and looked?"

"Sure I did. My land, isn't it?"

Imagine setting out across that field, under the bright country stars, with no more light than a good flashlight and whatever scrap of moon might still have been up, to see if an alien spacecraft of a type that has a reputation for kidnapping people might be sitting at the bottom of the hill! Could I have done it? Maybe. With the dog along. Curiosity is a powerful incentive, as many an ape has found, and ownership is sometimes even stronger.

Thinking of what that walk must have been like reminded me of something. "You didn't hear anything strange? Smell anything?"

"No-o-o-o," Miller replied, reflecting. "'Course, the smell of the ground and leaves is pretty strong this time of year, and there'd been a skunk killed out on the road; I noticed that Friday. Saturday afternoon I wasn't here, of course."

To my befuddled look, Miller said, "Stock auction. Bought my grandson a cow." In his old army shirt and bib overalls, he looked the part.

I nodded and got out my steel tape, pulled it out about a foot and set it gently beside one of the oval "bootprints" to take pictures. I shot several, from different angles and distances, freer now that I knew more film would be coming. After the fifth shot, I remembered my pocket compass and added it to the tape, and squeezed off a couple more frames. Gustafson and Rogers arrived back at the fence with the rest of the equipment.

"Karen's on her way," Gustafson said. "Shouldn't take her long."

"She wanted to leave the equipment we weren't using in the car," Rogers complained. "Very careless attitude. I warn you, Jamison, if anything goes missing, it'll be your responsibility. I had a break-in at my old apartment despite the precautions I took. I know better, now." He glanced at what I was doing. "Oh, good. You've got a ruler. I was going to remind you of that."

"You know what we don't have, though," I said. "Casting plaster. I'd like to get casts of these prints."

"Plaster of Paris do?" Miller asked. "I got some up to the house."

"I think so. I don't really know much about taking casts of prints," I admitted. "Does anyone else?"

No one did. "Call the sheriff and ask," Rogers said.

"Oh, now," Miller said, "you don't want to go bothering the sheriff."

"Call him," Rogers said. "He's a public official."

After a little more argument, Miller went up to his house for a bucket of water and the plaster, leaving Rogers to grouse about stubborn hicks. A minute or two later, Gustafson set out after Miller. While they were gone I took pictures of the oddly fused ends of the fence wire—I noticed that the little green men, like Miller, had left the bottom wire uncut—and clipped off several inches of each wire for the sample bags.

A *hmp!* of surprise from Rogers distracted me from the fence. "Got some radioactivity here," he said.

Odd how that word, *radioactivity,* can raise a little thrill of alarm, all by itself. "Much?"

"Not really." Rogers moved his scanner back and forth a few times. "Above background, though, and only inside the circle."

"So whatever caused the circle caused the radioactivity?"

"Looks that way."

The alarm died abruptly, washed out by a wave of excitement: I noticed that the grass was trampled past the cut in the fence, and I could actually distinguish some more of the little oval prints.

"No disturbance in the magnetic field," Rogers reported. "Where's Gustafson? I want him to take notes."

"He walked up to the house." I gritted my teeth over my excitement and set the tape down beside one of the impressions in the dry grass. A nightshade berry had been crushed into it. I took a careful picture and looked for the brownish stain in other prints and found it in the second one closer to the road. "I've got the outward trail here," I called to Rogers. "It's pretty clear, even in all this brush. I'm going to follow it. Coming?"

"In a minute."

I looked up and saw Miller coming over the crest of the hill with two buckets and a sack. Around one arm he carried something I'd totally missed thinking about: a tacked-together wooden frame to use as a mold around the prints.

Rogers set down the instrument he was using and gave the pressed-down circle a wide berth to join me. "Watch out for that bottom wire," I warned him.

"I've got eyes." He stepped over the wire, his just-cited eyes searching the ground along the path the prints had taken. Again I had that sense of coiled energy, as if he were a stalking beast.

I left him to stalk and met Miller to make sure he didn't cross the landing circle with the bucket of water. "Took me a couple of minutes to find a plastic bucket," he apologized. "Don't want to let plaster set in a galvanized one, it's hell to get out. Then I thought about this"—he held up the wooden form—"and that took me a couple minutes more. Sorry if I held things up."

"That's fine. Glad you thought of it."

"Jamison!" Rogers shouted. "Quick, bring the camera!"

Can't just be more footprints, I thought as Miller and I headed toward him. *Some kind of artifact?* I swallowed my eagerness again and stepped over the one wire of the fence Miller had left uncut. With the farmer right behind me, I circled around a blood-red clump of sumac to avoid stepping on the part of the trail I hadn't photographed yet. A flock of yellowish birds dining on sumac berries took to the air, yelling *tseet, tseet!* Distracted, I almost broke my neck when I caught my foot in an old gopher hole.

Rogers squatted beside a line of trampled grasses and weeds, his elbows on his knees, staring at an object on the ground in front of him. "Somebody's done a dissection," he announced.

The object had once been a rabbit, or a major part of one. Ants had been at it, and flies, but they were only minor latecomers. I stared at it for about ten seconds, and then I heard a choking noise close to my left shoulder and turned to see what it was.

Herman Miller, dead pale, with his eyes tight shut and one fist pressed against his mouth to keep from throwing up. Thinking of that midnight walk across his field, I bet you anything.

III

KAREN ARRIVED WITH the film five minutes later. "Where's Ed?" she called, as she picked her way toward us.

"Gone to the high school to ask the principal if you can talk to some of the witnesses there tomorrow," Miller said shakily when she reached us.

"Ick, what's that?"

"Bits of a bunny-wunny," Rogers told her. "Go back to that supermarket we saw on the way over here and get us some bigger plastic bags." He wrinkled his handsome nose at the sick-sweet stink of the rabbit. "And make it fast."

Karen shot a glance at me out of the corner of her eye and took a breath. "You're very welcome," she said, turning back, but Rogers didn't appear to hear.

The sun was low enough that the remains of the rabbit were in shade. I put the flash on the Minolta, wondering what kind of grisly pictures I'd be facing when the prints came back. The comfortable putter of a light plane passed to the west as I set up, casting an instant of deep shadow. I wondered if the pilot could see the bunch of us standing over the rabbit, and what he'd think if he knew what it was.

"Could we hire that plane to take an aerial shot of the landing site?" Rogers wondered aloud.

Miller shaded his eyes and looked toward the small craft. "I don't know. The airport's a ways away and I don't know anybody with a plane," he said.

"It's pretty low, isn't it?" Rogers asked.

"They come over that way all the time."

Rogers went back to his examination of the rabbit. After a minute or two he stood up. "Fire away," he instructed.

Fire away. Birdies and bunnies season. "This thing couldn't have been dropped by a hunter, could it?" I asked Miller, who

22

had taken my notebook to write down the technical details for each of my photos.

He laughed, a weak little sound. "I can see you're no hunter yourself," he said. "No, a hunter would have gutted it, maybe even skinned it, but he wouldn't have done it like this. Not split the head open like that, and to gut it he'd just have made one long slit in the belly."

Rogers nodded. He'd moved into the sunlight now, hands in the pockets of his still-immaculate jeans, and stared down at the rabbit as I planned my shots, his square jaw working back and forth.

"And he wouldn't have just spilled the guts out like that and left it," Miller continued. "Not a decent hunter, anyway."

"And a hunter wouldn't have taken samples of the small intestine and the colon," Rogers added. "Or half of the brain. I wonder why only half?"

"Is a rabbit's brain split down the middle, like ours?" I asked.

"Yes, but still . . ."

"Maybe they were short on room, so they thought they'd take only one of what looked like two similar things."

"In that case, why take all the lobes of the liver? The whole thing's missing. And why take the femur? That's not the easiest bone to get loose, especially in a wild rabbit with strong tendons. You'd think they'd take the whole leg."

"Or the whole rabbit."

"Or the whole rabbit," Rogers said, the first simple agreement I'd heard from him.

"I've got another question," Miller put in. "What was it killed with? I don't see no trap marks, and you'd have seen if somebody put a slug or pellets in it, right?" Rogers pulled at his lower lip and nodded, speechless for once.

We left the unfortunate cottontail where it was and did some other work while we waited for Karen to come back with the plastic bags. Miller went back to his barn to make some more wooden molds, and I mixed some of the plaster and spooned it gently into one of the footprints with the small mason's trowel I'd found in one of the buckets.

"Try to avoid getting any bubbles in it," Rogers advised me. "I want a perfect cast."

Karen would have said, "Yes, master," or maybe even "Okay, do it yourself." But I'm me, and I just clenched my teeth. A minute or two later Rogers was telling me how fortunate it was that he'd thought of taking the casts, and I kept quiet about that, too; I didn't want to ruin the investigation with a ridiculous squabble over territory, not when it was beginning to look like the best case I'd ever encountered. Off in the distance, I could hear the snipped screams of Miller's table saw as he cut wood for more forms, and I contented myself with fantasies of running Rogers through the saw, as I leveled the top of the plaster and watched for rising bubbles.

By sunset the remains of the rabbit had been transferred to a plastic sack and then to the cooler. We had pictures of everything we'd found, and casts of all the footprints cooling in a row. Miller had made another trip back to his house for a second sack of plaster before he excused himself to feed his hogs, and I'd put a couple of plastic bags over my shoes and taken casts of the three depressions in the larger circle. Karen and I were just finishing up the soil samples, with Rogers buzzing around us giving a lot of unheeded advice, when Ed Gustafson turned up to see how we were doing.

"Hey, let me take those," he said, reaching for the grocery sack of samples. "I know a guy at Carleton who'll analyze them for us."

Rogers pulled his chin back and stared at him. Maybe he thought it was funny that a farmer would have connections at a well-known college, but I've met enough UFO enthusiasts not to be surprised at anything they come up with. Rogers, though, hung onto the grocery bag until he got the name of the man at Carleton, and even then he was obviously grudging when he turned the bag over to Ed.

I said, "Careful. They're radioactive."

"Kidding." Gustafson pushed his cap back and scratched at his right temple. "A lot?"

"No." I repeated what Rogers had told me. Gustafson wanted

to see the needle jerk for himself, so we rescanned the circle in the twilight.

"How about that." Gustafson stuck his hands in his back pockets and regarded the circle, silvery now in the evening light. "Well, don't worry. I got some lead-foil pouches once just in case something like this ever happened." Rogers narrowed his eyes and stroked his chin, a gesture a guy I used to share an office with called "drawing the evil out of my heart"—meaning that he was giving in to suspicion.

But Gustafson looked as open as ever. "How about us getting some dinner?" he asked. "I'll take you all out to that Home Kitchen I was telling J.J. about."

Three quick acceptances; we'd all skipped lunch. "I'll just stick these in the back of my truck and stop by home to get those pouches around them," Gustafson said. "Meet you at the Kitchen in maybe forty-five minutes—that long enough?"

"Sure," said my stomach, through my mouth. The four of us picked our way through the weeds to the truck and the station wagon. Ed took off, and Karen directed me to a little road not far ahead where I could turn the boat around without going into a ditch or getting broadsided by somebody in a country hurry. I shook my head. It didn't seem possible that at seven-thirty that morning I had walked out of my office to check with a couple of engineers on what they planned to do this week.

"Well, what do you think?" Karen closed the door to our room and cocked her head at me.

"I don't know," I confessed. "I've never come across anything that looked remotely this good before, but I'm pretty leery about saying, 'Yes, this is it.'"

"Is that why you let that jerk talk to you like that? To keep the peace and get the job done?"

"Something like that."

"Only filthy-rich and down-and-outs talk to each other like that," Karen remarked, as if she had no use for either group. "Me, I'm middle-middle-class, and I can't stand it."

"I ought to be able to keep a grip on my temper for two lousy days," I said doubtfully, lying back across the bed. "Especially with you here."

"I'm glad I came," she said, looking at me in the mirror as she ran a comb through her hair.

"So am I. For one thing, you've been a real help, running those errands, for which great thanks."

She sighed. "I could stand not being ordered around, but that's not your fault. Do you think I should put on a skirt for this Home Kitchen place? Ed seems to think it's pretty special."

"You look fine the way you are."

"My good slacks, then." She unsnapped and unzipped her jeans and pushed them over her hips in one continuous swift motion. "Aren't you going to get out of your grubbies?"

"I'd rather watch you."

"Joe!" Karen slapped my hand. "You said *watch*. And I do think you should change your pants, at least. Ed will be waiting already."

So I changed into a fresh shirt and slacks, plugged in my razor and ran it over my chin, combed what's left of my hair, and was pronounced fit to be seen with. Tired and hungry, I decided to take the car even for such a short jaunt. We collected Rogers and were on our way almost on time. As for time, Rogers had used his well; more of the aftershave, and a sleek, fresh-from-the-valet outfit of slacks and sport coat that made me feel scruffy all over again.

The Home Kitchen marked its presence with a large black-on-white sign that, with the help of a row of spotlights, both assured us of fine food and pointed the way to the parking lot. I followed the arrow and was surprised to see that we were by no means the only customers, even on a Monday in October. I deposited the wagon next to Ed's pickup and we got out into savory air.

At first glance, the restaurant looked to be an old farmhouse. Close up, the building had clearly been designed for its purpose; inside we found a small bar and a large, not very brightly lit dining room. No sign of a kitchen. A fair number of people were dining, giving an undercurrent of conversation and cutlery to the soft background music.

26

"Should have worn the skirt," Karen muttered.

A trim hostess of thirty-five or so in a silky black dress that would have needed a lot more buttons to go to a funeral picked up three menus and moved languidly toward us. She greeted us with a demure smile, though her eyes traveled slowly twice the length of Cameron Rogers's tall body. "Smoking or non?" she asked, like hostesses everywhere in Minnesota.

"Non," Rogers said.

"We're meeting Ed Gustafson," I said.

Her smile widened into an all-out grin. "Oh, you're the guys checking out our UFO! Hi! Ed's over there in the smoking section, but there aren't many people here tonight and he doesn't smoke, himself."

"Move him, then," Rogers demanded.

The grin disappeared. "Sure, if you feel that strong about it," she agreed, and strode across the room to talk to Ed.

"Pearls," Rogers said, over Karen's head.

"What?"

"She should be wearing pearls with that dress, instead of that dinky gold chain. Give you a little more to think about, know what I mean?"

I didn't, right off, but he told me: I was supposed to be thinking about the string of pearls breaking and falling down inside the neckline of the dress. Then some nice guy could make a friendly offer to retrieve them.

Karen gave Rogers an indescribable glance and turned her back. The hostess, trailed by Ed Gustafson, came toward us. I wasn't sure whether to watch her approach or not, not with Karen beside me looking at my face, because Rogers was right about those pearls, damn it.

The menu was short, varied, and not too expensive—a pleasant surprise. A less pleasant surprise was the conversation that followed an excellent meal.

"Awful lot of work setting that up, wasn't it, Gustafson?" Rogers remarked, sipping coffee. The eyebrow went to work again.

Gustafson's big hands came down to rest at the sides of his dessert plate. "What do you mean?"

"That so-called landing."

I watched Gustafson's color drain and flood back. His fists tightened. "What's that supposed to mean? That it's somebody's idea of a joke?"

"Exactly."

"Wait a minute," I said, thinking of the radioactive dirt. "What—"

"Butt out, Jamison."

My own fingers twitched. "Sorry, I'm part of this too," I said. "And if you've got some reason to think this is a hoax, I want to know what it is, because I haven't seen it yet myself."

"That's the trouble with this whole flying saucer mess," Rogers sighed. "I've been fighting it for years. Every single damn report gets investigated by incompetent fools who can't see what's under their noses. People with some technical training, maybe, that makes them think they're whizzes at everything, but with absolutely no sense of what a scientific problem requires. All they do is muck up whatever evidence there is."

If he hadn't sounded so sincere, I'd have belted him. Karen's hand came to rest on my wrist as Rogers patted his lips with his napkin and put it beside his plate. "What tells me is that rabbit," he said.

I hung onto my temper, for Karen's sake and because Ed was hanging onto his. "What about it?"

"Point one." Rogers stabbed the table with his forefinger. I almost expected a hole to appear in the tablecloth. "It was autopsied in a very human manner. Now, hunters may gut an animal by cutting a single slit, but when you're trying to preserve the integrity of the internal organs, one way is to first make a transverse incision along the costal margin—"

"Whoa," Gustafson said. "What's that?"

"Cut along the edge of the ribs," Karen said, before Rogers had quite opened his mouth. He glanced at her with a flicker of surprise and interest.

"Go on," I prodded.

28

"Yes. Cut along the edge of the ribs, if that's how you want to put it, Karen, and then down through the center, one layer of tissue at a time, so as not to cut into any of the organs. That's the way this rabbit was done. And—my second point—the organs taken were the important ones: liver, spleen, stomach, kidney—just one of those—heart, lungs. Portions of the intestines. Half of the cerebrum and the brain stem. Now, I ask you, is a naive investigator likely to happen upon precisely that combination of samples? When he doesn't know anything about the functioning of those organs? For all he knows, the most important part of the rabbit is the fur!" He grinned at Karen. "I know some people think it is."

Put like that, it did seem strange. Gustafson must have thought so too, because he picked up his coffee cup, looked at it surprised, and set it down. Empty.

"Not only that," Rogers continued, "but that rabbit's skull was cut with a bone saw. Now, how likely is it that the person who did that happened to find a bone saw hung on a bush?"

"Not on a bush," Gustafson said, working his fingers. "In the saucer."

I swayed back toward neutrality.

"Speaking of bones," Rogers added, "that could be why the thigh bone was taken. To conceal the fact that it had been broken in a trap."

"I didn't get a look at it," Gustafson muttered. "But it's mostly lower joints that get caught in traps."

"And on top of all that," Rogers said, with the air of a bridge player producing the ace of trump to claim the setting trick, "there wasn't more than a smear of blood on the ground under it. Now, have you ever cut up a rabbit without any blood coming out of it?"

"Maybe when it was old," Gustafson said slowly. The words ticked off something in the back of my head, something my buddy Mack Forrester had said once, talking about a murder case he had been working on. But the waitress interrupted with refills on coffee before I quite got hold of it, and it was gone.

"Wait a minute," Gustafson said as the girl left. "What if this wasn't a—what did you call it—naive investigator? What if—"

"You mean those livestock mutilations?" Rogers interrupted, sounding exasperated. "Wild animals, or rustlers, or Satanists, for all I know. Perfectly earthly causes. No one has ever proved—"

"But nobody has ever disproved, either," Gustafson insisted. "Haven't there been rains of blood and meat reported too?" His voice rose over Rogers's immediate protest. "And if these aliens have been cutting up animals for years, of course they'd know how. If what you said is really a good way of doing it, don't you think they'd have figured it out after all these years?"

I could almost see Mack in the recliner in my family room, leaning forward with his right forefinger tracing out his explanation on his left palm in that way he has. . . . Got it! "We can at least tell if the rabbit was in the same position we found it in for a while right after it died," I said.

"How's that?" Gustafson looked interested, Rogers more than a little distrustful.

"A friend of mine, a cop, told me once about something called 'postmortem hypostasis.' It actually leaves a stain on the skin. Seems that after the heart stops pushing it around, blood settles to the lowest part of the body. You can tell that a body's been moved when the settled blood isn't on the bottom when you find it—I guess after a certain amount of time it gets stuck where it settled. Why can't we look for that in the rabbit and see if it was moved?"

"Jamison." Rogers, who had been nodding thoughtfully only seconds before, recovered himself. "A rabbit is covered with fur, hadn't you noticed?"

"We can shave it, can't we? I hereby volunteer my very own electric razor. And if that doesn't tell us, we can skin the damn thing and look on the inside."

"Right!" Gustafson slammed his right hand on the table. "And we'll take pictures all the way. Will that suit you, *Doctor* Rogers?"

Rogers sighed. "I suppose."

Gustafson settled the bill and we trooped back to the parking lot and sorted ourselves into the truck and the car, ready to convoy back to the motel and shave a dead rabbit.

"I'm glad I had the shrimp Celestine," Karen remarked, as Rogers slammed his door. Nasty of her; Rogers had ordered hassenpfeffer. But then, he must have had a cast-iron stomach anyway.

IV

CHECKING A BODY for hypostasis is a little like doing blood tests in a paternity suit, only the other way around—a blood test can't prove that a man *is* a child's father, only that he couldn't be, and examining hypostasis can't prove that a body *hasn't* been moved, only that it has. In the case of our rabbit, we were left wondering. The deep red suffusion, almost like a blush, matched the position we'd found the poor beast in, down to a pale pressure mark exactly where a large twig had been lying under the body, but the idea of somebody sitting in the bushes cutting up a rabbit on a bright Saturday afternoon seemed unlikely, especially to Rogers. He and Gustafson didn't exactly agree to disagree—I don't think Rogers was capable of that—but Gustafson, after pointing out that neither hide nor muscle of the disputed leg had been mangled by a trap, shut up without giving in. There the matter was left.

Rogers himself must have felt some doubt about his stated position, because when I insisted that we still should interview the witnesses to the Saturday night visitation, he agreed without protest. We tucked the rabbit away in the cooler with the test tubes and went to bed.

Tuesday morning the sun chased a band of mauve across the sky and claimed it for blue, not the painful blue of the day before but a soft, fall color exclaimed over by a *V* of geese that passed high to the east. Karen put on her skirt in some sort of deference to visiting the high school, but kept her loafers, and she and I walked to an early breakfast at the Home Kitchen (which had suffered an overnight character change from black-without-pearls to folksy gingham), relieved to be rid of Rogers for a while. An hour later, stuffed with bacon, eggs, and pancakes, we strolled slowly back through the cool morning, along a path so wide and smooth it must have been made intentionally to connect the motel with the restaurant. The brush beside the path was alive with small birds; Karen picked a late aster and twirled it between her fingers as we walked. Near the motel we met Rogers, on his jaunty way to breakfast, and said the shortest possible hello.

We'd arranged with Ed Gustafson the night before for him to come and lead us to the school in his pickup, and not so incidentally to act as our credentials. We'd been back in our room about half an hour when he came by. Karen capped her pen and put aside the notebook she'd been writing in, and the three of us lazed in the room, talking about this and that, with an eye on the window to see when Rogers returned.

Karen had just shut the bathroom door behind her when Ed remarked, "Well, here comes the bastard himself." He sat forward and put his hands on his knees, shaking his head as he prepared to get up. "I never saw the like in all my life, did you?"

"Not often."

Rogers must have noticed Ed's truck, because instead of going to his own room he pounded on our door. "Ready to go, I see," he said, when Ed let him in. The man seemed almost jovial; after the night before I couldn't figure it out. He rubbed his hands together and continued, "Let's hope for a profitable morning, gentlemen. As I have every reason to believe it will be—but it will have to wait a few minutes while I call my lab." He crossed the room to the telephone and dialed the front desk.

"I know what room I'm in," he said a moment later. "Just place the call, will you? That's your job." Gustafson rolled his eyes. We sat looking at each other trying not to overhear what Rogers was saying, an impossible effort.

"Okay, Bucky, what went wrong yesterday?" he began. "What do you mean, nothing? There's always something. What kind of results did you get?"

He listened for a moment. "Of course I know it's still incubating. I just wanted to be sure you knew it should be." I got up and went to the window, and Gustafson wandered out to his pickup. That left me stuck; Karen was still in the bathroom and she sure wouldn't appreciate coming out to find herself alone with Rogers.

"Stupid people," he muttered, banging the phone down. "Have to keep an eye on them every minute. Turn your back and God only knows what will happen."

Karen came out of the bathroom and cast a startled eye at Rogers. "Oh, are we ready?" she asked. She was looking especially trim in silk shirt, tweed skirt, and woolly vest. Rogers examined her with a smile that made me want to stuff my fist in it, and bowed her past him.

Once again she got into the back seat. I drummed my fingers on the steering wheel as Rogers took his time getting some notecards from his room, toying with the idea of leaving him stranded.

"Don't," said Karen, who occasionally reads my mind. "The pleasure wouldn't be worth the hassle."

I'd been too enthralled and too busy the afternoon before to take note of traffic on the road beside us, and I was startled to find that it was the road between Fox Prairie and the larger town where the regional high school was located. As we went past our site, I craned my neck to see if the circle was still undisturbed, but a clump of scrubby trees was in the way as we came down the slope from the north, and the blob of sumac cut off the view as we whipped past. Driving, I couldn't turn around to look at the spot from the other direction, so I just crossed my fingers.

Ed had spent a lot of time bragging about the high school's special programs in math and physical science and the science club's big grant for some kind of nuclear physics project, and the building wasn't nearly as big as I had expected. "Oh, it's just over three hundred students," he told me when we'd parked in a lot reserved for teachers and guests.

We pushed through old-fashioned heavy wood-and-glass doors into the lower hall. Size made no difference to the chalky, floor-wax smell of the place, so familiar as we tramped through the rubber-tiled halls that I almost felt as if I should have a hall pass from a teacher.

34

When I'd called the principal to make sure he knew we were coming, he'd responded warmly with a rich, deep voice like a singer's. So his appearance was a shock. Short, a bit on the dumpy side, with a small chin and the mouth that sometimes goes with it, where the fold of the upper lip extends onto the cheeks to give the whole face a faintly pouched look, he didn't look anything like the vague picture already formed in my head. His little eyes kept flicking sideways under their droopy lids to assess Cameron Rogers. God help the man if he was measuring himself against a guy who looked like that!

"Oh, I assure you, I have all the confidence of these kids," he said to Rogers when Rogers objected to his sitting in on our interview. "I'm also the football coach, you know, and we've won our first three games. Made the class-C finals last year too."

"That's a good record for such a small school," Karen remarked. "You must have your team pretty well organized."

"Oh, yes, yes." The principal smiled, tucking the corners of his mouth under the folds of skin. His face looked somehow unaccustomed to the act. "But my boys are what does it. Hard workers, every one of them, yes, indeed."

He fussed us into a little room we could use for our interviews and called to the clerk to find some extra chairs. "Aren't you staying, Ed?" he asked when Gustafson excused himself.

"No, I got work to do. Between this and the election, I've let too much slide already," Gustafson said. He handed a large brown envelope to Karen. "Here, you take charge of this. Don't open it yet, though."

"Sure you don't want to stay, Ed?" the principal asked, although Rogers was steadily driving him out of the little room by standing too close.

"Nope. Got to run." The principal, whose muttered name I hadn't caught, turned to me as he took another backward step. "A fine man, Ed Gustafson. They don't come better. That's why we elected him president of our club."

"Club?" Rogers repeated, momentarily halting his maneuver. I thought, *Kiwanis, maybe, something like that.*

"Our UFO discussion group. We were very interested in your

article, Dr. Rogers. We devoted an entire meeting to it, back last summer when the paper came out." Stepping through the door, the little man finally acknowledged what Rogers was doing. "Sure you don't want me sitting in? It might make the kids more comfortable."

"Absolutely."

I'd been about to invite him to stay, and I glanced at Karen to see what she thought. "I think I'll wait outside too," she said. "Is that okay with you, Coach Stemmermann?"

"Sure, sure," the principal said. "Maybe you and I could even discuss this landing. Quite a day for little Fox Prairie, isn't it?"

Small-town kids don't seem to change. The trappings change: Walkman radios, grungy jeans, even a startling green hairdo had been in the halls as we'd passed on our way to the office. What doesn't change is the pecking order, the social slots the kids assign themselves to. We got, one at a time at Rogers's insistence, the football hero; his girlfriend the head cheerleader; two grinds and a Boy Scout who had been on their way to a science-club meeting at the advisor's home; a fast girl (I thought several times about reminding Rogers that she was barely fifteen, but to judge from her perfume, she knew perfectly well what she was broadcasting); the jock who'd taken the fast girl to the movies; and the French and Latin teacher, a volatile-looking brunette with a tough veneer for the kids that she slipped off as if she'd shed her coat when the door closed behind her, and that she slipped right back on after two minutes with Rogers.

Somehow our interviews with the boys all took the same pattern: me interested, friendly, just the way I felt; Rogers asking hard, insulting questions that made one of the grinds snarl and stalk out of the room. With the girls and the French teacher, Rogers turned silky and suggestive, which left me squirming. Still, we got answers, and when we put them together, the magazine Rogers had thought would be interested might have written the story like this:

On a cool, clear Saturday night near the beginning of October, life in Fox Prairie, Minnesota, went on much as usual. In a home near the center of town, Jeannie R. was combing her long honey-blond hair, waiting for Gerard "Spook" K. to pick her up. They were planning to take in a movie in a nearby town. The movie was an old one, *War Games,* and Jeannie had already seen it at least ten times. She kind of liked the guy in it—he reminded her of Mark O., a boy who sat ahead of her in English class and seemed to know all about computers.

Mark O. himself was preparing to leave the house where he lived with his parents and three sisters. He was planning to attend a science-club meeting at the home of the club's advisor, and he was to pick up two other club members and drive them the seven miles to the meeting. At about 7:15 he backed his ancient Fiat 1100 out of the driveway of his parents' home and headed for his friend Bob's house, frowning over a strange new sound in the engine. The third club member, Steve H., had walked over to Bob's house and was waiting with him on the front-porch steps to avoid the attentions of Bob's two small brothers.

Chuck K., Spook's cousin, had picked up his girl, Mary Ann W., after football practice. They'd had a burger and fries at a McDonald's near the school and had stopped at a friend's house for a few minutes, which stretched into hours when they decided to play some games on the friend's Atari.

Miss N., the French and Latin teacher at the high school, had decided on the spur of the moment to spend one last weekend with a man she was dating at his summer cottage near Fox Prairie. But the weekend was sliding from bad to worse: as Chuck and Mary Ann were finishing their burgers and Mark was honking his "eloquent two-tone klaxon" (as he called the car horn, after the description in the owner's manual), Miss N. and her boyfriend were heading into a spat. The quarrel continued for nearly an hour.

Miss N.'s altercation with her friend reached a height at approximately 8:30. She slammed into her brand-new red Ford Escort and sped through downtown Fox Prairie toward her own home near the regional high school. By the time she had driven a couple of miles through the cool October darkness, her anger had faded and she was merely glad she had left, so that when the sighting began she was more curious than upset.

About four miles south of Fox Prairie, as she topped a rise in the road and headed downhill, Miss N. noticed a bright red light off the road to her right. Her first thought was that it might mean someone in distress, although the light was too big to be a taillight of a vehicle. She slowed down sharply. The light moved about with a strange bobbing motion, very near the ground, so that she thought for a moment it must be carried by a child. Then she noticed that there were no other cars near—she had thought she might see one stalled on the shoulder of the road—and as she neared the light it suddenly went out.

Even though she was raised on a farm and is not normally a nervous person, "My hair just stood up on my head," Miss N. reported later, "and I jammed my foot on the gas and got out of there." As she arrived home, her telephone was ringing. The caller was her boyfriend, apologetic now that he'd thought things over, and she talked to him for "quite a while" without mentioning the light.

The next to see the strange light were Chuck K. and Mary Ann W. As they were changing game cartridges at the friend's house, Mary Ann suddenly remembered that she had promised to be home to watch her younger sister. It was then nine o'clock. "I called my mom, but the line was busy," Mary Ann explains. "I figured she was calling around looking for me, and since I didn't want to get grounded for the rest of my life, I made Chuck take me home right away."

As the two neared the dip in the road that Miss N. had passed less than half an hour before, they, too, saw the red light—in this case, off to the left, because they were traveling in the opposite direction. "It was real low and kind of bouncy," Mary Ann says. "When we came over the hill, I thought maybe a kid was jumping around with one of those flashlights with the red around the front, but then I saw the light was much too big, like the size of a basketball, maybe."

Chuck wanted to stop and investigate, but Mary Ann, mindful of her angry mother and (she now admits) a trifle frightened, pleaded with him not to. He compromised by passing the spot at a crawl. Just as the car came opposite the light, it went out.

"I can't explain it," Chuck says. "It was just—I dunno, creepy. Yeah. So I floored it and got us out of there." (Chuck, it should be noted, is a fullback on the championship high-school football team, elected captain by his teammates and noted for his toughness and cool head under pressure.) "Couple hundred yards down the road a rabbit crossed ahead of me—I saw the eyeshine bouncing across the road—and I about peed my pants."

The pair arrived at Mary Ann's house to discover that it was on Sunday, not Saturday, that Mary Ann had promised to baby-sit. They told their story to Mary Ann's mother (her father is not living at home). Considering their agitation, Mrs. W. suggested they call the sheriff's office and report the incident, which they did. The call is logged at 9:55.

No one seems to have thought it necessary to investigate the single report of "a creepy light by Miller's place," and no car was sent out.

Shortly after that, Miss N., having patched things up with her boyfriend, headed back toward Fox Prairie again, this time accompanied by her dog, a beagle named Snoopy. As she neared the spot where she had seen the red light, she found herself peculiarly unwilling to drive past it, but since that is the only road that leads to Fox Prairie, she had no choice. As she approached the top of the hill, her dog put his forepaws on the dashboard and stared out the windshield. Sure enough, as she reported later, "When I topped that hill, there it was again, just about where it had been before. Snoopy let out a howl—God, I can't tell you how it sounded. I didn't even slow down that time, I just scooted." Miss N., busy with her reconciliation, didn't immediately tell her friend of her experiences. When she did, it was nearly an hour later.

Meanwhile, the movie had lost its interest for Spook and Jeannie. Since it was a cool night and Jeannie's parents weren't expected to be home until after eleven, the couple decided to go to her house and "watch a little television." At a little past ten they started the gentle downhill slope to the dip in the road where three people had already seen the mysterious light, one of them twice.

"I saw it first through the bushes," Jeannie reports. "And I knew it was too big to be a flashlight, but it was too bright to be anything else I could think of, except maybe one of those plastic Halloween pumpkins the little kids carry, you know? Only it was red. So I went, "Hey, Spook, what's that?' "

Spook pulled the car onto the shoulder about sixty or seventy yards up the hill. When they had first seen the light, it had been bobbing around, but when they stopped the car, the light stopped too. "Like it was looking at us, you know?" Spook says.

"Like it noticed we'd stopped and it was waiting for us to do something," agrees Jeannie.

After a brief conference, Jeannie and Spook decided to go on—but with a difference. Spook was driving his father's Honda, and his father kept a powerful flashlight in the glove compartment. So Jeannie took the flashlight and climbed into the back seat, where she could sit on the left side of the car, and got the light ready. Spook started onto the road again and drove on slowly. Just as the two high-school students were about to pass the light, it went out.

"I kinda forgot where it was, but I put the light on anyway," Jeannie says. "I didn't see anything real definite, you know, but there was one shadow of something short and black and *gross*. I mean, I really, really freaked out! I just screamed, *Spook, get out, it's coming for us!*" As she recounts this, Jeannie's eyes open wider and stare at something beyond the wall of the small room where she is talking.

"I got," Spook says. "Man, was I ready!"

As planned, they drove on to Jeannie's house, but instead of watching TV they talked about their experience. Jeannie had the certain feeling that they had come upon something strange, "Like an ET, only not nice. Or some kind of ghost." Thinking her parents might have an explanation, they waited for them to come home. By that time it was quarter after eleven; although Spook and Jeannie had seen the fourth appearance of the light, theirs was the last call to the sheriff.

The science-club members left their meeting about 9:30. During the meeting, which had been called at that odd hour and place in order to make some astronomical observations, the club members had watched a red light, low in the sky to the north, soundlessly drifting downward. At the time it was dismissed as a light aircraft, but now the three who traveled together have cause to wonder.

At the time, with no suspicions, they merely stopped at the McDonald's near the school for a snack. They left for Fox Prairie at approximately 10:20. They had the same experience as those before them: approaching that field of Herman Miller's, they saw a light bobbing in the bushes between the field and the road. The trio decided to stop and find out what it was, Mark remaining in the car to keep it running, since it was often hard to start.

As the car rolled to a stop on the shoulder, the red light went out. The boys discussed this phenomenon in whispers for a moment or two. Bob and Steve were in favor of shutting off the engine and keeping quiet to see if the light might go back on, but Mark vetoed that idea. "I didn't want to have my head under the hood and maybe get grabbed by something out of the dark," he explains. So it was decided that he would stay in the car with the engine running, and Steve and Bob (an Eagle Scout) would go find out what the light was. Steve suggested it might be swamp gas, but Mark reminded him that it had been a very dry fall and that the field wasn't in a damp spot anyway, since it was drained under the road into a small creek on the other side. Bob agreed—he thought the light was far too bright for swamp gas, in any case, and with the clear sky it couldn't be ball lightning.

The only flashlight available had a beam yellowed from much use under the hood of Mark's car, but it was better than nothing, so the boys got out with it and prepared to cross the road. At Steve's suggestion, Mark shut off the headlights. "I don't know if you know about country nights," Steve told this investigator. "There wasn't a moon, but there was plenty of starshine and our eyes were pretty well dark-adapted. So we stood by the car for a minute and whispered about where the light had been. We decided to split up and approach the spot from opposite directions, with Bob shining the light and me looking to see if I could see the shadow or silhouette of anything."

They followed this plan, each of them walking perhaps fifteen yards along the road in opposite directions, then crossing the road and turning to walk toward one another. Bob took a couple of steps and turned on the flashlight.

"Instantly there was this *huge* flash of light," Steve says. "It was directed straight at Bob. He kind of staggered and went, "Steve, help, I'm blind," so I went running to him. At the same time I heard something crash in the brush to the side of the road. That's the wide side, you know, where the right-of-way is if they ever want to widen the highway."

Scared, Steve pulled Bob across the road to the car. Bob's hands were pressed to his eyes and Steve was afraid they might have been burnt, "like from looking at the sun."

"Mark, we gotta get Bob to the hospital," he called. Mark turned on the headlights, revved the engine, and the car stalled.

Now thoroughly frightened, the boys locked themselves in the car while Mark tried frantically to get the engine started. All Bob could do was to huddle in the back seat with his hands over his eyes. Steve tried to keep a lookout on the other side of the road, but while some of the verge farther ahead was lit by the car's headlights, Bob had dropped the flashlight and Steve couldn't make out anything near where they had seen the red light except a few weeds dimly illuminated at the edge of the ditch by the yellowing beam. He remembers his heart beating heavily as he tried to see if anything might be crossing the road behind them, possibly visible against the thick stars.

At last the starter motor brought the car to life and Mark, his heart in his throat, wrestled the wheel all the way to the left and made a quick turn in the road to head back the way they had come. Nothing out-of-the-way showed in the headlights as they swept over the brush. A car came over the hill behind them, and Mark was relieved to have company. Steve, watching out the back window, reported that he could see nothing in the road that shouldn't be there, though he thought he saw the headlights of the car behind them glint on something in the bushes.

"Don't stop," Bob pleaded. "Don't stop. I don't want another flash like that."

Mark saw that the other car was slowing down at the dip in the road. "I hope they don't get hurt," he groaned. "Are they stopping?"

"I don't think so," Steve reported. "No." As they crested the hill, the other car seemed to be following them, and a third had appeared at the top of the other rise. "I wish they'd come along a little sooner," Steve complains.

By the time they reached the next town, Bob's vision was clearing, so they decided to go straight to the sheriff's office at the county seat instead. The drive took twenty minutes.

Miss N. and her boyfriend had become friends again, and she told him of her experience with the two spooky lights. Intrigued, he suggested that they go see if the light was still there. Ten minutes later, after the three boys had come and gone, they, too, drove past the spot. Miss N. had taken her own car; engrossed in watching the side of the road, she missed seeing a motorcycle coming and nearly swerved into it when it passed her with one glaring eye. To her sudden, unexpected disappointment and her friend's amusement, no red light was to be seen. In vain, Miss N. pointed out her dog's uneasiness. Another quarrel threatened, and since the friend couldn't get out of the car at seventy miles per hour, both of them went to the sheriff's office to report the red light, arriving about five minutes after the boys.

With all these people in the office, and the call from Jeannie and Spook coming just then, the dispatcher finally decided to send a deputy to investigate. The deputy, knowing Ed Gustafson's interest in odd phenomena, picked him up on the way, and the two of them drove to the dip in the road. The deputy shone his spotlight over all of the brush for a distance of fifty yards, but saw nothing. Whatever it was had gone . . . leaving behind a landing imprint that wasn't discovered until the next morning.

"Quite the little story," Rogers remarked, knocking his notecards into a neat stack as our last witness shut the door behind her.

"They seem sincere."

" 'A little sincerity is a dangerous thing, and a great deal of it is absolutely fatal,' " he said. "Pushes a lot of garbage down your gullet if you don't watch out."

Seven earnest young faces, and one older one that didn't seem to know how to wear its nervousness. "You don't think eight people put this story together, just for us?"

"Why not?" Rogers leaned back in his chair. Both eyebrows went up, somehow not nearly so infuriating as the nearly sub-liminal flick of one that I'd almost come to expect. "Jamison, you've been in this game long enough to understand the hick mentality. They *love* to put one over on the city slickers, haven't you learned that?" He chuckled. "If you'd been with me at breakfast, you'd know Fox Prairie isn't the innocent outback it pretends to be," he added mysteriously. "The conversation was not at all about our UFO."

"What do you mean?"

"Never mind. As I said, nothing to do with this." Rogers chuckled again as he twisted a rubber binder around his cards and put them into his jacket pocket.

Damned if I'd be drawn. I flipped back through my own notes. "The stories all mesh," I said.

"That's just what makes me suspicious," Rogers announced.

"They mesh. Smacks of collusion." I wondered whether, if they hadn't meshed, he'd have taken it as an indication that they just hadn't gotten their act together, but this was Rogers, and I had promised myself not to get into any arguments. "Think about it, Jamison. All our witnesses conveniently clustered in this one school."

"We came here to interview witnesses from the school," I pointed out. "And it's natural they'd talk about what they'd seen, especially since the principal is interested in UFOs."

"I wouldn't be surprised if it's that dwarf of a principal behind it all," Rogers replied. "And they put men like that in charge of children! Somebody ought to complain to the school board. I might, myself. Well, let's get going. We've wasted half the day."

More than half; school was about to let out. My stomach was rumbling again—I'd paid close attention to those references to a McDonald's near the school. Rogers flung the door open and marched out without looking back. I checked that we hadn't left anything behind, turned out the lights, and shut the door. Karen stood against the wall opposite the room.

As she stepped toward me, Coach Stemmermann came out of his private office with a small smile. "Well, Mr. Jamison, did you get what you came for?" he asked.

"Yes, thanks very much." I shook his extended hand. "I appreciate your setting this up."

"A pleasure, Mr. Jamison, Mrs. Jamison. Come on back sometime when you have time to discuss UFOs with me. You must have some fascinating stories to tell." He tucked up the corners of his mouth and made a little bow. It wasn't until we were halfway down the ringing iron stairs that I realized he hadn't said a word to Rogers.

44

V

"You know what's in these, don't you?" Rogers asked as I bit into my hamburger.

Oh, no. "What?"

"Beef." He grinned. "Probably imported. You're eating the rain forests of South America." He took a bite of his own Big Mac. "With ketchup."

Karen set her hamburger down on its box and pulled a few french fries out of a sack emblazoned with yellow arches. "And the potatoes are fried in lard," Rogers went on. "So if you're watching your cholesterol, take it easy." Evidently he wasn't watching his own.

Karen shot me a quick sideways glance. *She* watches my cholesterol, when I can't talk her out of it, with profound attention. "I like lard, for the flavor," she commented. "I always use it in pie crust. That's a trick I learned from my roommate in college. Could she cook! She won a bunch of blue ribbons at the Ohio State Fair."

Maybe Karen does use lard in pie crust, for all I know. I can't remember the last time she baked a pie; she also watches our waistlines. Her own mild expansion is a source of grief—to her only. I like it.

Rogers shut up for a while and finished his french fries. We collected ourselves, after he'd paid me back for his lunch out of an overstuffed wallet, and started back toward the school parking lot four blocks away.

This town, although built of the same tan and maroon bricks, was significantly larger than Fox Prairie: on the way to lunch, I recalled, I'd noticed someone peering through a drugstore window on which was posted a schedule of bus runs to Minneapolis, a service the smaller town didn't have. For that matter, I couldn't remember seeing a drugstore in Fox Prairie. Here I'd seen a

45

couple of clothing stores, a big hardware store that called itself an "emporium," a barbershop complete with striped pole turning outside the door, a variety store, and a place that sold sporting goods, all clustered a few blocks from a busy grain elevator. The sidewalks weren't crowded, but they existed, and people were walking on them.

Halfway to the school we passed a volunteer firehouse of jaundiced-looking brick that squatted in a billowing frame of chrysanthemums of at least a dozen colors, every one of which clashed with the color of the building. Rogers said something uncomplimentary about the taste of the Ladies' Auxiliary. Two doors farther on, Karen stopped to admire a couple of hand-thrown pots on display in a tiny shop window.

"American primitive," Rogers sniffed. "Just the kind of thing you find out in the so-called sticks."

"Exactly!" Karen's voice warmed. "Isn't it wonderful what you can find hiding in these unexpected little nooks?"

Rogers chuckled. "You'd be shocked at what some of these little nooks have hiding in them."

"Oh, I've found some wonderful things," Karen replied. "Things that would have cost four times as much in Minneapolis."

"You have?" Rogers sounded taken aback, but he recovered quickly. Why Karen had decided to spar with him I had no idea, but I recognized the technique. She calls it verbal judo: if somebody tries to hit you, shake his hand and help him fall down. Was she trying to drive him away? But we had the transportation.

No use speculating. Karen makes sense in her own good time. "You know," she said when we had once again arranged ourselves in the station wagon, "I think I'd like to take another look at that landing site, before it gets all trampled. Can't we put off checking that timetable with the sheriff's office until tomorrow? It shouldn't take long—we could still be home by noon."

"I don't see any point in going back to the site," Rogers objected. "In fact, as far as I'm concerned, checking out this incident at all is a waste of time. That bunch of jerks at the

46

school got together to put one over on us, and I'd just as soon give them the finger and go home. I've got other fish to fry."

I bet, I thought. A school bus blocking the exit of the parking lot moved aside and I nosed the car out onto the street. "I've never heard of a hoax involving more than two or three people before," Karen mused. "Not unless they were related. It's almost worth documenting just for that aspect, isn't it?"

"I'm not in this for pop psychology," Rogers snapped.

"Still . . ." Karen let her voice trail off. I recognized this technique too, and tried not to smile.

"Oh, all right. Suit yourself," Rogers said sourly.

A little relieved that I'd remembered my turns, I spotted the sign for Fox Prairie and swung right past an array of John Deere implements onto the county road. "Do you think a psychologist would find the case interesting?" Karen asked. "I hadn't thought of that. I was thinking more in sociological terms, if in that direction at all. Actually, I'm most interested in how they did it."

"Not worth spending the time on," Rogers declared.

"If somebody tries to put something over on me," Karen continued sweetly, "I like to know exactly how they planned to do it, don't you? And there are a few things here I confess I don't understand. Like how they made the ground radioactive."

"You'll find they have a special science program at the school," Rogers said. "Either that, or Gustafson's friend at Carleton is in on it."

"Is that likely?" Karen let the sentence sit in the silence for a minute or two. "Then, too, how did they compress the dirt in the circle like that, and what was that red light? And that flash—some kind of weapon, do you think?"

"An ordinary flash gun." Rogers didn't bother to veneer his irritation with what's usually called patience. The effect was oddly intimate, and I bristled. "If there was a flash."

"Two honor students and an Eagle Scout," I put in.

"I don't think they'd lie, do you?" Karen said. "And even out here in the sticks, I'm sure they'd know what a flash gun is. They've got all those video games in that arcade across from the school, I bet they've heard of cameras, too."

I wished Karen were sitting more toward the middle of the seat, so I could see her face in the rearview mirror. Her voice was just a little too neutral for comfort. "Karen—"

"They must have spent hours on it, if you're right," she remarked, as if I'd said nothing. "I wonder how they kept from tramping down the weeds, all those people?"

"My dear Karen, it's just not worth the time and effort to track down all their little tricks." Rogers turned sideways to face her again; he was grinning. "If we go away now, after a while they'll write us a nice ha-ha letter and we can say thank you, we knew it all along."

"Well, in that case, rather than waste your time, why don't Joe and I just put you on a bus for Minneapolis?" Karen offered.

Ah-hah!

"Then we can check out the landing site, see whether Ed's got anyone else to interview, and go back tomorrow."

"Never mind," Rogers said. "If you're that determined, I suppose I can find the time to stay with you and make sure you don't commit any irreparable blunders."

I have a feeling Karen lost interest in the landing site at that precise moment, though I've never asked her. The dip in the road appeared ahead; I saw stringy white clouds, like those that come before a rain, gathering in the sky to the northwest. "It'll be rained out tomorrow," I said. "Looks like this is our last chance. Did you bring the camera this morning, Karen?"

"It's in the glove compartment." She sounded bleak.

Gravel crunched under the tires as we pulled up across the road from Miller's field. I sat for a moment looking at it. The landing site itself was hidden behind a hodgepodge of red and yellow leaves and the pale tan stalks of weeds and grasses. A squarish hump the same color as the gravel interrupted the shoulder of the road some distance farther on: probably one end of the culvert one of the science-club kids had mentioned. A matching hump marred the smooth shoulder on this side, twenty yards from the station wagon's nose. The "creek" the boy had mentioned was dry, a mere fold in the field to our right. In spring, it might be as much as a constant trickle of meltwater.

Which of us made the first move, I don't know, but we got out almost in unison and closed the car doors quietly, as if slamming them might disturb something. Rogers licked his lips. "You don't think Miller's still here with his gun?" he asked nervously.

"Dunno," I said, and called out, "Miller?"

No answer. A few crows in the field behind us complained about the loudmouth who had had the nerve to disturb them. *"Miller!"*

We waited a few seconds in silence. No answer. We waited for an old blue pickup to pass and I started across the road, Karen close behind me. Rogers waited by the car. To see if we'd get ourselves shot, most likely.

"This must be about where those two boys were planning to meet." Karen stared first into the brush beside the road, then down at the gravel she was standing on. "Too tracked up to find any trace of them. That little blond girl said the light was behind some bushes, but it can't have been the sumac—it's too dense to let her judge the size or shape, don't you think?"

I glanced at her, puzzled. How did she know all that? We'd discussed the interviews over lunch, of course, but only to say what had been seen, and I was positive we hadn't discussed anyone in connection with any one piece of evidence. But Rogers's feet—now that safety seemed assured—sounded on the gravel on our side of the road; Karen put her finger to her lips as if in thought, and examined the ditch. "You know, we forgot the bags," she said. "In case we do find something." She turned on her heel and crossed the road to open the tailgate of the station wagon.

"We did all this yesterday," Rogers complained.

"Well, you can wait in the car, if you want," I said. "Karen and I can manage on our own."

"No, no. I'll stay." His fists were balled in his pants pockets, jingling his keys and his change, and the catlike energy was back. He bounced lightly on his toes as we waited for Karen to come back with the plastic bags. Meanwhile I walked up the road and glanced into the mouth of the culvert; it was actually just a large pipe, and of interest only because of the huge, tattered, but still-beautiful spider's web spun across most of the opening.

As I returned, Karen came across the road with a red box of bags in hand, the other holding the Minolta out to me by its knotted strap. "Let's start with the edge of the road," she said. "If anyone carried a lot of stuff in to set this thing up, we ought to be able to find some traces."

"You're sure we need to do that." My anger flared at Rogers's mocking tone, but Karen seemed perfectly cool. She moved slowly along the edge of the shoulder, her eyes on the ground at her feet. The sun slanting across the field turned her light brown hair into a cloud around her head and brushed a line of gold down the side of her skirt. Rogers began to whistle through his teeth.

Karen tucked her skirt behind her knees with a practiced gesture and squatted down to study something, something she picked up and put into one of the plastic bags. She stuffed the bag into her blazer pocket and continued her stroll.

"The landing is that way, Karen, dear," Rogers called after her.

"Yes, but that little dirt road is this way."

I left Rogers to whistle and caught up with her. "What was it?"

"I'm not sure, but it could be more of that rabbit." She pulled the bag out of her pocket and handed it to me. Something that looked like a tiny reddish-black stone was nestled in a lower corner. Pressed between the sides of the bag, it gave slightly.

"A dried clot?"

"Could be. Don't tell my mother, but I find things like that, only softer, in the refrigerator once in a while."

We continued our slow progress, while Karen examined the brush to our right. Once she balanced on the brim of the ditch and stared into the tangled quackgrass, but she came back shaking her head. "I thought someone might have walked through there, but it looks more like a dog or cat went through the grass," she reported.

"Or a rabbit?"

"I don't know. What do rabbits do for a living, besides eating our lettuce and tulips down to the roots?"

"You're asking me?" The ground tended uphill somewhat; now the end of the drainage pipe that carried the ditch water under the graveled end of the dirt road came into view, the top of it broken down and rusted. "You keep looking along the edge, okay?" I suggested. "I'm going to jog up to that road and see if I spot anything from that end."

The distance was only forty yards or so, not far enough to make me wish I'd worn my running shoes. When I looked back, Rogers was sauntering toward Karen, hands still jammed into his pockets. She waved me on.

In the hard flat midwestern sunlight the tracks of the station wagon in the little road were clear, though no one could have told exactly which vehicle had made them—shallow depressions in the gravel and the grass beyond it, the eight curving V's showing that the wagon had backed into the track four times, a different distance each time. Another, single track had reversed farther along the small road, where it bent to the south past a stand of small trees. Beyond the wide band of brush that bordered the highway, the gravel petered out and the dirt trail became just grass-grown ruts that forked, one set running beside the rusted fence of what looked like overgrown pasture and the other angling west along the edge of the field I already knew. Porcelain rings on the posts of the overgrown field suggested that the wire might be electrified; I avoided it and looked instead at the field where the "saucer" had "landed."

Rusted barbed wire, with one bright new section showing that the fence was kept repaired, edged this field also. It wasn't insulated. Miller's harrow had run within inches of the fence, but even so, as I walked toward it to look back past the small trees at the landing site, a bunch of fat little birds burst from cover and whirred along low to the ground, to become instantly invisible among the motley tans and browns.

The bold double track of a tractor crossed the field on an angle toward the new section of fence, and Miller's heavy boots had flattened the grass near each of the posts. The tracks of the tractor led to—or away from—the lower level of the field, near the highway, where the landing had taken place. New wire gleamed in the afternoon sun in the two damaged sections: Miller had repaired the fence today. I waved at Karen, who was standing at one end of one of the new sections, but she didn't see me.

Tuesday. Sighting along the edge of the field, I couldn't see any footprints or flattened grass. But anyone who walked there was being very careful, I reminded myself, and in three days even dry weeds can spring back somewhat. Green growth still pushed upward under the tangle of tan stalks. I followed the fence back along the little road, hoping for something, expecting nothing.

I found a thread caught on a barb of the wire. Olive-drab wool. I took the plastic bag with the blackened object in it out of my pocket and carefully folded it around the wool thread and jammed it back, well down.

"Found anything?"

Rogers came the other way along the fence. Karen trailed him, her face a blank mask of fury. She smiled briefly at me.

"Nothing here," I lied.

"Good, then let's get out of here." Rogers did an about-face and marched toward the main road. I tucked my arm around Karen and followed, much more slowly.

"What was it?"

"A little thread," Karen said through her teeth. "A little greenish-brown thread, caught on a sumac twig near where that rabbit was. I was just about to put it into a bag when he took it away from me and shoved it into his pocket. Where I hope it breeds lint," she added, so savage about it I almost laughed.

"I've got one from the fence," I whispered.

"Ah!"

We had reached the corner of the field. Karen paused and looked along the fence parallel to the highway. The weeds were full of little trails, none of them big enough to have been made by a man. It struck me that a careful man could have used one of them to disguise his own track, pushing the weeds apart and letting them fall together behind him while he balanced his

52

steps on the center of the trail. But far too many of them crisscrossed the waste ground to search in less than a whole afternoon, and Rogers had nearly reached the road.

He glanced over his shoulder. "You still want to hang around?" he demanded.

"Just a little longer." Karen jumped the ditch and stepped onto the shoulder of the main road. "I want to take one more look at the circle."

A van had pulled up behind our station wagon, a dark blue one with a sunburst in the rear window. "Who the hell is that?" Rogers asked with distaste. "Some panting spectator, I suppose."

As we drew closer, the man in the van opened the door and jumped out. "J.J. Jamison," he shouted. "Just the guy I want to see!"

A smallish man, with a chubby face and fair, curly hair. When I'd first met him, last summer, he'd reminded me of a photo of Dylan Thomas Karen had once shown me. Still did— and a writer of sorts, himself; Jackson Powell, the reporter who had interviewed me for the story in the Sunday paper that had eventually brought us all down to Fox Prairie.

Powell glanced both ways and trotted across the road, camera bouncing against his hip and a tape recorder clutched under one arm. "Hi, Doc," he said to Rogers. "So you're here too. Didn't recognize you without the white coat. Great. Let me get some pictures of the two of you looking at where this thing landed—"

"I beg your pardon," Rogers interrupted frostily. "I am Dr. Rogers, not 'Doc.' And as for pictures, no saucer landed here. It's a hoax."

"No kidding?" Powell's almost-invisible eyebrows rose. "Great, even better. I can get the two of you pointing out why it's a hoke-up, and—"

"Not I." Rogers folded his elegant arms. "I have already been the victim of your incompetent reportage once, and I have no intention of allowing it to happen a second time."

"What do you mean, incompetent?" The change in Powell's voice brought Karen a step closer to me.

"I thought I had made it clear in my letter to your editor that I resented having words put in my mouth."

Powell glanced at me and his own mouth quirked. "Aah, I thought what you said could use a little livening. And J.J. here has a better way with words, so I just didn't make it clear who said what. Sorry if I mashed your tiny toes."

What about my toes? I wondered, but Karen had her hand around my left elbow now and looked up at me with something like fear in her eyes.

"I seriously considered suing your newspaper for defamation, are you aware of that?" Rogers demanded. "I put that in my letter. I also suggested that you be fired, but I see that had no effect."

The quirk left the reporter's mouth, and the slight amusement died out of his eyes. Karen clasped my arm a little tighter. "Let's not argue about it," I said. "If Jackson wants a story, I'll give it to him and you can stay out, if that's the way you want it."

"Oh, no." Rogers swung around to glare at me with something like a snarl. "I've done an incredible amount of work on this case and I'm not going to let it go *that* easily! I've made castings of footprints, searched a hundred-yard circle around the site, tested for radioactivity and magnetic disturbances, interviewed a bunch of pimply kids, one of whom stank—"

That would be Jeannie, I decided. Half a bottle of Avon's best poured over her cuddly little body. Rogers hadn't seemed to mind this morning.

"—I've arranged for soil samples to be tested, and I have even done such ridiculous things as shaving a rabbit—at your imbecile instigation, Jamison. And if you think all that is something you can just take over, you'd better think again, because it isn't going to happen, is that clear?"

"Now, wait a minute." I felt Karen stiffen as she inhaled. "In the first place, *I* did the searching, such as it was. You never thought of it, hotshot. And in the second place, Joe made the castings, and you never thought of doing that, either. And in the third place, Ed Gustafson arranged for the soil samples to be sent to *his* friend at Carleton. You did damn all, except look at that rabbit. And it was even Joe's shaver that got all clogged up with fur!"

"Horse shit!"

Good God, I thought. *Can he really believe what he's saying?* Powell, wearing a huge grin, lifted his thumb to show me the little orange light on his tape recorder, spinning merrily along.

"You know what I think?" Karen plunged on, without taking her eyes off Rogers. "I think *you* did all this, so you could quote-unquote discover it was a hoax and get your name in the paper as the mighty debunker!"

"Where's the landing site?" Powell inquired, still grinning. "Down that way? I'll just need a couple of pix. I've got my story."

"I'll deny it," Rogers said, his jaw tight.

Powell waved the tape recorder at him and laughed.

The guy never had a chance. Rogers stood a head taller and outweighed him by ten pounds, all of it muscle. Before Powell could even react, he'd been jumped. He fell to the gravel with an *oof* of pain, hugging the recorder to his chest.

I tried to go to his aid, but Karen still had hold of my arm and she set her heels and jerked backward with all her might. I stumbled and went down.

Rogers had straddled Powell; now he pried at the recorder with one hand while he slapped the reporter over the ear with the other. Cringing, Powell put up a hand to protect the ear. With a yell of triumph, Rogers yanked the recorder out of his grasp.

"Karen, let go," I pleaded, trying to get to my feet. But she'd wrapped her legs around mine, and I watched Rogers carefully pin each of Powell's hands with his knees, eject the cartridge from the recorder and pull the tape out of it yards at a time. Not a damn thing I could do about it. "Damn it, Karen, get off me," I urged.

"He's crazy, can't you see that? Stay out of it, *please,* Joe."

Now Rogers had the camera. He twisted the lens off and threw it into the brush, popped out the roll of film and ripped it from the cartridge, tossed the bright yellow cartridge after the lens. Then he calmly rocked to his feet, grinding Powell's hands into the ground as he did so.

After a few seconds Powell also climbed to his feet, a little shakily and breathing hard, and rubbed the gravel-printed backs of his hands. A smear of blood covered the left one. "I'll get you for this, Rogers," he said softly. "I'll get you."

"Oh?"

The syllable invited a punch in the mouth, but Powell resisted. "Let me *up,* Karen," I pleaded.

"Please, Joe? Let them handle it?"

Powell snapped the back of his camera shut and picked up his tape recorder. He took a deep breath, blew it out, and glanced warily at Rogers before bundling the tangle of ruined recording tape into the side pocket of his worn corduroy jacket. "That's assault, *Doctor* Rogers," he said. "You know that? Assault, before witnesses."

Karen hissed as if she'd been burned.

"I don't think I need worry. Do you really want to be any more embarrassed than you already are?" Rogers sounded almost solicitous; my ears burned at the idea of being associated with him. Karen untangled herself to let me stand up, and I helped her to her feet. I don't think Rogers had taken the least notice of what was going on behind him.

Powell glanced out toward Herm Miller's field, in the direction his camera lens had taken, and then he shrugged and crossed the road to his van. He didn't look back once as he started it, backed up enough to swing around the station wagon, and drove off in the direction of Fox Prairie.

Rogers said, "He won't bring charges. They never do," with the confidence of a man who has bullied his neighbors since toddlerhood. "Are we finished here?"

Karen inhaled audibly. "I have a couple more things I want to see," she said.

"I'll wait," Rogers replied. Amiable. *God.* He dusted off the knees of his slacks, put his hands in his pockets, and sauntered along the shoulder of the road, whistling.

"Karen, for Christ's sweet sake, what do you want?" I whispered. "Let's just get out of here."

"I want to find the rest of that poor man's camera," she said. "I think I saw just where it landed." She struck off in a line toward the patch of weeds where the lens had disappeared, and cast a "Coming?" glance over her shoulder. Rogers still dawdled along our side of the road, kicking gravel with each step. I followed my wife.

She had stopped just short of the weeds. "Look at this," she whispered, pointing.

A thin drift of dirt from a new gopher hole had spilled across one of the little trails in the grass. Half of another of the oval footprints was bluntly outlined in it. And right next to it, exactly as deep, was the lengthways half of a print of an ordinary shoe, as if someone had stepped out of one and into the other. A sprig of grass was trying to poke its way through the instep of the print, but in the slanted sun the shape of the sole was still clearly outlined in shadow and gold. Karen looked toward the road, searching for Rogers. "He's going the other way," she whispered. "Quick, get a picture."

I took three, with my watch for scale, calling down blessings upon the inventor of the automatic-exposure camera. When I looked up, Karen had moved on and was parting the weeds where she thought Powell's lens had fallen, working slowly over the whole area. "Did you notice?" she asked. "The weeds were beaten down a little back there, like someone had set down a lot of stuff."

"Yeah, I saw that."

"And something else. That print's just about the size of yours. It can't have been Rogers's; his feet are too big."

"*Not* Rogers?"

"Shhh!" Karen moved a little to her left. "Maybe it was more over this way." She continued parting weeds to look for the lens, leaving me to wonder who else in this charade wore a 10½C shoe. As I stared thoughtfully at an odd blue reflection among the weeds I became aware that I was looking at the back end of a camera lens.

"Got it," I called softly. On examination, the lens didn't seem much the worse for wear. It had landed lens cap down, and only a bit of crumbled dry leaf from the weeds had fallen into it. I blew the dust out and dropped the thing into one of Karen's plastic bags for safekeeping.

Driving back to the motel, with Karen once again in the back seat and Rogers in front, I thought I knew how terrorists feel as they speed toward their targets with the live bomb on the seat beside them.

Only I wanted to get home alive.

VI

KAREN CLOSED THE door and leaned against it, her head tilted back against its glossy brown surface. Her face looked pale and drained. After a moment her throat swelled as she swallowed, and she opened her eyes. "Joseph," she said. "I absolutely can *not* ride fifty miles tomorrow with that man in the car."

"I'll say." I slumped onto the edge of the bed and rubbed my fingers over my scalp, which was having a good shot at squeezing my brain out through my ears. "I'll drive him over to catch the bus in the morning. I think the last one's already gone for today."

Karen peeled her back away from the door and collapsed onto the edge of the bed beside me. "Some little vacation!" After a few minutes of glum contemplation of the ruins of her getaway plan, she wriggled her shoulders and said, "Say, I have another piece for our puzzle. Where Miller cut the fence to let us into the field? He's got that fixed, I guess you noticed. Where he trimmed out the wire in that section, the cut ends of the old fence are shiny-bright, not a speck of rust. But that part where the saucer people supposedly cut the fence, where that's cut back there's a film of rust over the ends of the old wire. What does that mean?"

"Obviously, it was cut earlier." Karen took over massaging my scalp and it loosened in gratitude. "You know, we never did measure that cut section to see if that wire really belonged there," I mused. "It was there, so I assumed it always had been. Dumb."

"You can't think of everything." Her thumbs ran firmly over the muscles of the back of my neck. "You think somebody cut that section out and stapled in a new one, already cut in the middle with those funny ends?"

"Could be." I paused to consider what was necessary. "I'd

59

hate to carry around all that barbed wire myself, but it would be a hell of a lot easier than lugging an acetylene torch down there." I rolled over and put my arm around Karen, but she slipped away.

"Hold your horses," she said. "Jackson Powell's van was in the lot when we came in. I want to let him know we've got his lens."

Having been told to hold my horses, I obediently thought about other things while Karen dialed the desk and asked to be connected with Powell. Such as: How had she known what Jeannie with the honey-blond hair had said about the light behind the bushes, or what the two science-club kids had planned?

"I'm almost ashamed to talk to you," she said into the phone. "But I want to let you know we've got your camera lens. . . . No, Joe and I looked for it. . . . Sure. How's your hand? . . . Oh. Gee, I—no, I was sitting on him." She rolled her eyes at me and I began to be distracted again. A slight shift of her shoulders let the lamplight outline the curve of her throat, except where the shadow cast by her collar was split by a small streak of light through the buttonhole. I reached out, and she caught my hand and pressed it down to the bed. "Well, he is my husband," she said, with the exaggerated patience of exasperation. "Because I wanted to get your lens back to you. . . . Sure, I think Joe would be willing. When? Before dinner? . . . That place up the road is pretty good. . . . Yeah, it's got a bar. Okay, we'll see you."

"Phew!" Karen hung up. "By way of apology for not stripping that ape off his back, you're going to give Powell an interview," she told me. "I hope you don't mind too much."

"Not since it doesn't have to be right away," I said. "My horses just got their bits in their teeth."

"Oh, that's right." Karen grinned at me and started to unbutton her blouse. "Our vacation."

Half an hour later, I remembered what I had been thinking about just before Karen had started talking to the reporter. "Kay," I said. "How did you know Jeannie was the one who talked about seeing that light through the bushes?"

Karen giggled. "Stemmermann listened to the whole thing on the intercom, didn't you guess? Said he'd never been this close to a real UFO case before and he wasn't going to let some snotty Ph.D. cut him out of it."

I pictured the tiny, windowless room, with the one long table on one end of which we had worked and on the other end of which textbooks had been stacked a yard high, near the wall. "He hid the intercom behind those books?"

"Right." Karen rolled onto her side to grin at me. "Oh, I can't wait to write up some notes on that guy! What a character! He said he figured from something Ed Gustafson had said that Rogers might take that attitude, so he set it all up in advance. Invited me to listen along. Ordered all his calls held. You'd be surprised how many calls a high-school principal can get in the course of a day."

Looking at Karen wasn't helping me think clearly, so I dropped onto my back and folded my arms behind my head. The interviews ran in flashes through my mind, the cheerleader looking scrubbed and preppy, the wide shoulders of the mouth-breathing fullback. . . . "He must have heard what Rogers said about him, then," I mused. The man hadn't even looked at Rogers as we were taking our leave.

"Did he ever!" Karen confirmed. "He was livid! Muttered something about having enough trouble already without that jackass making more."

"Trouble? Did you ask what he meant?"

My wife favored me with a look of total scorn. "Of course I didn't. As it was, he looked at me as if he was shocked that I was still there, so naturally I pretended I hadn't heard."

"I wonder what he did mean?"

"Don't know." Karen fell silent for a minute or two. "Rogers!" she said suddenly. "I absolutely cannot figure that guy. Did you catch that quote from Wilde? I bet he meant every word of it too."

"Quote from Wilde?"

"That bit about sincerity. Didn't you recognize it? I think it's from *The Importance of Being Earnest*."

"No, it went right over my head," I admitted.

"What time is it?"

I picked up my watch from the bedside table and squinted at it. "Almost six-thirty."

"Oops! We're supposed to be meeting Jackson Powell, and I haven't even had a shower!"

"Maybe we shouldn't have walked," I said. I reached for the long brass door handle. "It'll be dark by the time we're done eating."

Karen held up her handbag with a smile. "I've got that keychain flashlight if we need it," she said, a little out of breath from our fast pace. I looked over my shoulder as I held the restaurant door for her. The clouds that had been just starting down from the northwest as we drove toward Fox Prairie earlier that afternoon now covered the sky with a uniform gray sheet from horizon to horizon; I hoped it wouldn't be raining as well as dark by the time we headed back to the motel.

My eyes took a few seconds of adjusting to the dim light of the bar before I spotted Jackson Powell sitting in the corner of a deep booth along one side. He was wearing the same jacket he'd had on that afternoon, brown corduroy rubbed smooth at elbows and pockets, with drooping leather buttons. The left elbow had a small right-angle tear in it that looked new.

"Sorry," Karen said, holding out both hands as she approached him across the mottled red carpet. "My fault we're late. It felt so good to get into a shower that I kind of lost track of time. Have you been waiting long?"

Powell shrugged. "Twenty minutes." Long enough to have emptied the glass that sat on the table in front of him, and to have been sipping the meltwater off the ice until it was reduced to one small piece shaped like a figure eight. The back of his left hand had been patched with three strips of surgical tape; a few little spots of blood had oozed to the surface of the tape and dried a dull brown.

I said, "I'm sorry about this afternoon."

Powell shook his head like a surfacing diver and held up a finger for the waiter. "How in hell did you come to hook up with that bastard?" he asked.

"You did it," I told him. Karen slid into the dark booth and I slipped in beside her to face Powell. "With that story last summer. I'd met him maybe two or three times before Sunday, but if it hadn't been for Ed Gustafson reading that story, I'd never have come down here with him. Maybe not at all."

"My turn to apologize," Powell said. "What will you drink?"

"Beer will do." Powell ordered a Heineken, and for Karen her standard pre-fancy-dinner-out vodka martini, half and half on the rocks with a twist.

"First time I ever ordered a recipe," Powell commented, getting a notebook out of his hip pocket. He held it up. "That was my last tape he ripped up, too, so until I can pick up some more it's back to the nineteenth century." He flipped over several scribbled pages to a fresh one.

Karen took the lens in its plastic bag out of her handbag and passed it across the table. "Oh, I appreciate this," Powell said. "I was thinking I'd go hunt for it in the morning, but the way the weather's shaping up it might've been too late to save it." He turned the lens over several times, holding it near the feeble wall lamp in the booth. "Diaphragm still works," he announced. "Hope the thing's not out of alignment. Well. Thanks." He dropped the bag into one of his sagging jacket pockets. "Now, how about this mess? You think it's a hoax too?"

"I'm getting more convinced all the time." The waiter arrived with the order, and I watched him pour from a frosty green bottle into a glass. "Who did it and how it was done, I don't know, but yes, I think it must be a hoax."

"You sound disappointed."

I shrugged. "I wouldn't be working for CATCH if I didn't hope that someday one of these stories would turn out to have a grain of truth."

"What makes you think this isn't the day?"

I told him about the rabbit, and what Rogers had said about what was done to it. He got a good laugh out of the shaving scene—three grown men and a grown woman jammed into a cheap motel-size bathroom spreading a specially purchased issue of the local paper on the floor to catch the fur and the mites and the maggots, three of them taking turns retching into the toilet.

"Rogers is a cool one all right," Powell commented, mouth pursed. "What about this pressure mark?"

"That had me wondering too," I admitted. "But if you had planned carefully in advance, you could have set the thing up with a twig under it, ready to slide into place when you got it there."

"Have to check that. About as thick as a thumb, you said?" Powell outlined a bit of his scribble with a bold rectangle. "See if it's embedded in the grass, like it should be."

"Too late. Rogers picked it up."

"Not a country boy, are you?" Powell remarked. "The twig would've left an impression in the ground, too, if it really belonged there."

"Tell him about the fence," Karen urged.

"You tell him. That's yours." She did.

"Now, that is interesting." The tip of Powell's tongue ran over his upper teeth. "Yes. Nice. Did you happen to notice if the wire matched what was already there? The cut wire, that is, that you took a sample of?"

Karen and I stared blankly at each other. "Gee, no," I said. "Barbed wire is barbed wire is barbed wire, I thought."

A quick grin from Powell. "Not by a long shot. People even collect all the different kinds, mount 'em on boards and hang 'em on their walls. I did a story about that once. But the samples with the fused ends will be easy enough to compare with the old fence that's still there. I bet somebody cut out the section, bent the ends back to hold the rest of the strand—that stuff's put up under tension, usually—used a torch to cut the middle of each strand, and came back and poked the ends under the old staples. Probably spit on it to rust it a bit, so the fresh cut wouldn't be noticed. You didn't happen to measure the sections that had been cut?"

"No."

"The FBI will never hire you, J.J." Powell drew another rectangle around some more scribble. "Well, at least we can go look to see if the old staples have been disturbed. What else?"

64

"Wool thread." We produced our similar stories of finding threads caught on one sort of hook or another, and what had happened to Karen's find.

"I see why you think Rogers worked this up," Powell commented, writing. "I wonder if he's got an olive-drab shirt?"

"Half the country must," Karen said. "But I don't think anymore that he did it." She told him about the wrong-size footprint.

"He could have had an accomplice," the reporter pointed out. "That would explain a lot—like how he knew about the one place along that road where nobody could see the thing being set up. That's local knowledge, got to be."

Karen nodded slightly. "Oh," I remembered. "And the track. There's a little dirt road maybe forty, fifty yards south of the landing site, graveled, oh, twenty feet in from the main road. Besides the four times we turned our car in it, the gravel's got the mark of something that could be a motorcycle that was run in past the trees. One of our witnesses talked about nearly hitting a motorcycle when she *didn't* see the light at the landing site, her third time past."

"You've got witnesses to a light at the site?" Powell's jaw dropped.

"You didn't know?"

"No. I just got here this afternoon. Somebody from the sheriff's office called the paper and said there were weird things going on down here. My editor called your organization and the lady there said you were investigating, but she didn't have a report yet. I don't think she knew about the light either," he added, with just the accusatory tone Prunella Watson herself might have taken.

So we backed up, and I put the whole story into as much chronological order as I could. My glass was empty well before I was done, and Powell signaled for another green bottle to stand beside the first one. Karen shook her head when I was finished with the story.

"Joe," she said, "I've been sitting here counting and counting and I only get three times that we backed the wagon into that road. Once when I went back for the film." She grabbed her index finger with her left hand. "Once when I went to the supermarket, and once when we all left for the motel."

I stopped and counted for myself. "You're right."

"So what was the other car?"

"Ed Gustafson?" I proposed.

"He turned in Miller's yard," Karen reminded me.

"Somebody who had a lot of stuff to carry and didn't want his car noticed?" Powell suggested.

"It's hunting season," Karen said. "Nobody would think twice about a car parked along the shoulder."

"Unless it was a car that might be recognized, and didn't belong."

We sat and looked at that in silence for a minute or two.

"Here's what I think," Powell said. "Somebody who knew that Herman Miller would be gone Saturday afternoon took that time to set up the landing site. I had a quick look, before I cruised the road to see if there were other hidden places along it—like I said, it's the only spot along that whole road where you can't see into the field from the highway. All the impressions in the ground could be produced without much trouble. Some kind of padded board to break down the clods for the circle, something to strap on your feet for the little footprints— that gets you in and out of the circle without tipping your hand, or foot, maybe I should say. Then you make the so-called landing-foot impressions by mashing a bucket into the dirt—"

"They were placed in a perfect equilateral triangle," I pointed out. "That we did measure."

Powell shrugged. "Anybody can measure." He looked back at his notes. "The only thing I don't get is the radioactivity. How do you make the ground radioactive?"

"You're asking me?"

"The rabbit's no real problem. . . . " He frowned at his notepad. "Then you get rid of all that stuff and come back after dark with something to make a light with and that flash gizmo that blinded the Schultz boy. Then you sit making lights at people until somebody stops to investigate, and when they do, you shoot off your flash at them and they run away. That's taking a

66

chance, but it might be worth taking. . . . Jeez, if the sheriff had sent out a deputy on that first call. . . ."

He stopped and frowned again. "A deputy wouldn't run, flash or no flash. I don't like that, it's not as careful as the rest of the plan, but maybe there's something I'm missing . . . maybe if you could camouflage your stuff . . . ?" Powell ran down. "Well, I think that's the outline, anyway."

"Sounds plausible," I agreed. "Right now, though, what I want is dinner. You ready?"

"You guys go ahead. I'll get a sandwich from the bar and sit here and stare at this a little more, see if I can make anything jump out at me."

So Karen and I left him awaiting the spring of the beast. I glanced back into the bar as we left and saw him reflected in the rosy mirror behind the ranks of colored bottles. He was chewing his thumb. A few minutes later the hostess who didn't wear pearls seated us in another booth in the dining room with a big smile for the absence of Rogers, and we settled down to examine the menu.

The Home Kitchen changed its menu every night, just like Mom always did, but *my* mom, at least, never cooked like that. Whoever was in the kitchen could have made gourmet fare of creamed chipped beef on toast, but that wasn't on the menu. I ordered roast duck and dared Karen to stop me.

"We're on vacation," she said, smiling, and reached for my hand. "I'm having the pork tenderloin. We can run it off later."

For starters we were brought a yellow pea soup so good and so filling I began to hope they'd skimp on the portion of duck, and we were halfway into it when somebody stopped beside the booth.

"Would three be a crowd?" Ed Gustafson asked.

I glanced at Karen. "Not at all," she lied gamely, and Ed slid into the booth beside me.

"I don't ordinarily eat here twice in the same month, let alone two nights in a row," he said. "But you weren't at the motel and I wanted to talk to you, so what the hell." The waitress brought him a menu and he handed it back to her, saying, "I'll have whatever Mrs. Jamison is having," and the girl went away. "I figure what you're eating won't be as fattening as whatever J.J. ordered," he explained to Karen.

"Oh, dear. And I just ordered the pork, since we're on vacation."

"Some vacation!" Gustafson snorted. "A reporter name of Jackson Powell stopped me on the way in and did I get an earful! Some afternoon you had. Who'd have thought a Ph.D. would turn out to be a street tough?"

"You get all kinds anywhere," I said. "I've met a few engineers who weren't exactly the soul of congeniality. Some of those guys from the East Coast have their knives out as a matter of course—but I can't think of a standout like Rogers, not offhand."

"Herm Miller's father was a dyed-in-the-wool bastard, for one," Gustafson remarked. "Even his cows hated him. Died at a young age, he did." He looked up at the waitress, who was about to serve him a bowl of the pea soup. "Oh, Debbie, that's just what I need," he exclaimed. "I'm not used to eating this late in the evening."

"What did he die of?" Karen asked. Ed stared at her and repeated her last two words blankly. "Herm Miller's father."

"Oh." A good deal of the heartiness faded from Gustafson's face. "Got trampled to death by his dairy herd. Nobody ever figured out just how it happened. Herm got rid of the herd right after that, started growing corn and beans. It's only the last couple years he's gone back to any kind of stock, and it's just a few breeder pigs."

Karen looked at the last of her soup. "I wish you hadn't told me just before they were going to bring my roast pork!"

"Ah, well, we'll just have to find something different to talk about," Gustafson said, the bounce back in his voice. "What did you get from those kids at the school?"

Herman Miller. Why hadn't I thought of him before? He'd been just a figure standing around offering help when he saw it was needed, but it was his field the "saucer" had "landed" in, and who better to set up the hoax? He'd have everything he needed on hand: the barn must be full of stuff he could use to crush the clods in a circle; he'd actually handed me a plastic

68

bucket—maybe even the same one that had made the "landing pod" impressions!

Nice going, J.J.

Rabbits were all over the place, and if he'd grown up on a farm, for Pete's sake, he'd know how to make a rabbit look as if it hadn't been gutted by a hunter. . . . I shut my eyes against a grisly vision of the rabbit's head guided into the blade of the table saw I'd heard but never seen.

My duck arrived, thin rosy-gray slices with a rind of crisp brown skin, bedded on a plate with wild rice and some lettuce and stewed apricots that tasted of orange.

But the radioactivity? It always came down to the radioactivity. What farmer has something in his barn to make the dirt radioactive? You'd need a nuclear reactor.

Or a flying saucer.

"How's the duck, J.J.?" Gustafson asked.

"Super." I pulled a smile out of nothing, and pasted it on my face.

"Pork's good too," he said, forking some into his mouth. Karen nodded, her eyes on mine. She looked a little puzzled; I guess I'd been a lot quieter than usual. But then, I'm one of those guys who can't talk and think at the same time, which makes some people think I'm a lot stupider than I really am.

At least, I hope I'm not as stupid as I sometimes look. I suddenly realized that I'd completely ignored Ed's question about the day's interviews.

VII

THE REASON ED had asked about the interviews, it turned out, was that the envelope he'd handed to Karen at the school (another thing I'd completely forgotten) contained copies of the notes he'd taken from the witnesses himself, so we'd be able to compare their stories two days apart. A good idea. I appreciated his standing at the machine in the library feeding it dimes to make the copies, and I promised to read his batch of interviews as soon as we got back to the motel.

"There's five others in there," he pointed out. "Not connected with the school."

"Thanks." If the stories the high-school kids had told matched what they'd told me, and the others added nothing new, I figured I could ask them my questions by mail. "I've got another question for you," I said, as the waitress handed me the dessert menu. "Karen and Coach Stemmermann listened in on those interviews, I guess you know"—Ed chuckled—"and at the end of them Rogers had a few choice words about the coach; people like that shouldn't be in charge of kids, persuading them to put on a hoax like that, et cetera. Karen says he muttered something about being in enough trouble already. Is he?"

"Ah." The syllable was something between an exclamation and a gasp, and it spread Gustafson's mouth into a wide square smile that was no smile at all. To my surprise, his face began to redden. "Well, yes and no," he said.

I let him fiddle with his one remaining fork for a moment, waiting.

"You know that stuff up in Scott County, couple years back? All those people . . . and kids. . . . "

"Oh." Several cases of sexual abuse of children, some of which had made the front page of the city papers day after day—whole groups of children inveigled into "games" with a

70

few adults, some of whom were at it for years before some anguished kid finally told. I nodded.

"Well, there's this runt of a kid who didn't make the football team. I mean, he can't pass, he can't punt, he can't run or kick—nothing. Couldn't even carry the water bucket without slopping half of it down his pants, I bet. And the kid's father is a real go-go rooter for the high-school team—you know how it is with some people when there's really nothing much else to do."

The waitress came back and we ordered coffee. Gustafson took the opportunity to see who was in the booth behind him: no one.

"Anyway," he continued, "the kid said he was kept off the team because he wouldn't . . . you know. So the father called up every last member of the school board and blistered their ears, and George was called up to explain himself to them. What a shock! Can you imagine? Well, the whole team and some of the other kids who tried out and didn't make it testified to the board that nothing like that ever happened to them, and the kid who said it was already famous for telling stories. Then, when the county attorney was about ready to bring charges, the kid admitted it wasn't true; he was already a bust at hockey and baseball and now football, and with his old man a real jock, he was plain scared of failing again. But a lot of people figure, where there's smoke, there's fire, you know?"

"But, surely . . ." Karen stopped.

Gustafson sighed. "To top it all off, the kid got himself beat up in a fight beginning of last week, and now there's talk going around that it was because of what he said, that the boys who beat him up didn't want to stop . . . what he said they were doing with the coach. So now *those* parents are up in arms." He sighed again and slapped the edge of the table with his big hands. "I don't know. Sometimes I think the whole world's gone crazy. In my day, the kid who started it all would have had a few licks of the razor strap from his O.M. the day he opened his mouth, and that would have been the end of it." The coffee had come while he was talking; he drained his cup and slid to the edge of the booth. "Well, I'll leave you two to your vacation.

You going back tomorrow, or you want me to set up some of those other witnesses for you?"

"We'd just as soon go home. You got their addresses in the envelope?"

"Yeah. Maybe writing's a better idea, anyway. Well, thanks for coming down, J.J. 'Preciate it. Sorry you had to put up with Rogers."

I lifted a hand, and he nodded and skirted the tables in the middle of the room to stop at the cashier's desk. She got up and craned her neck, looking for the waitress, most likely.

My wife is prettier than the cashier and the waitress put together, so I looked back at her. "Alone at last," I said.

"Snatching a forbidden moment," she replied, not entirely joking. "Remember when we got married, Joe? Did you ever think it would be like this?"

I didn't know what she meant. "That we'd be eating in this restaurant?" I hazarded.

"No. That we'd have our privacy so picked at all the time." Her hands flopped at the edge of the table and she folded them in front of her. "I was a romantic, I guess." She nodded to the waitress, who had buzzed over to hover with the coffeepot, right on cue.

"Come on," I said, after the coffee had been poured. "It's not that bad, is it?" I felt vaguely defensive, as if I could have provided that privacy, somehow, if only . . . what, I didn't know. "Hey, since we're not driving, how about a postprandial brandy in the bar?"

She grinned. "That's right. Vacation. Take a little time to be naughty." There was a sardonic undertone to her voice I didn't like, but I called for the bill as if she'd simply agreed with me, left it on the table with enough to cover a tip, and we made for the bar.

Jackson Powell was gone, but Cameron Rogers was hunched on one of the bar stools. Karen silently pointed toward an empty booth that looked as if Rogers wouldn't be able to see into it from his perch at the bar. We sneaked across the noisy room like a couple of thieves and scooted into the leather seats, close to the wall. Karen had her giggling smile, though she didn't make a sound. "Pleasures newly found are sweet," she whispered.

"Is that a quote?"

"Wordsworth." She sighed and cocked her head at me. "Oh, Joe, I don't know how you managed to get a master's degree, I really don't."

"What do you know about tensors and vectors?" I asked.

"Not a thing. Funny, isn't it?"

"Happens all the time." I looked up at the waiter, who was standing at the end of the booth with a towel over his arm and his pencil poised over his order pad, as if he'd been there long enough to develop every one of the freckles that blotched his cheeks and forehead. "What kind of brandy do you have?" I asked.

"Martin, Coronet, Courvoisier."

"Two Courvoisiers," I ordered, proud of myself for figuring out what *cur-voy-zer* was.

"Show-off," Karen said as the waiter left.

"I bet the cook knows how to pronounce it."

"Ah, he's just a farm kid, what do you want?"

"Kay—"

Whatever I was going to say, it died in my teeth. Cameron Rogers, Ph.D., slid his centerfold body—clothed, of course; I'm only extrapolating—into the booth next to my wife.

"Who invited you?" I demanded.

"Me." Slow, fake smile, higher on one side than the other. "Look, I want to apologize for losing my temper this afternoon," he said, his speech a shade slurred. *Just remembered we've got the car,* I concluded. "I've already talked to Powell and made my peace with him. I'll buy him new lens and film and tape, and he'll forget the whole thing, just as I thought."

Karen opened her mouth and closed it. How much would a new 50mm. lens cost at, say, National Camera Exchange? Sixty bucks? Less than my *per diem* when I traveled for the company. My estimate of Jackson Powell went down a couple of notches.

"Lemme buy your drinks," Rogers said, dragging out his bulging wallet.

"No, thanks," Karen said. "This is a private celebration."

Rogers nodded, but if he recognized a signal to leave, it didn't take. Karen cast me a desperate glance.

"Look," I said. "Karen and I were having a private talk, and we'd like to continue it. So, if you don't mind?"

Rogers could have had a seatbelt on, welded shut. He put his elbows on the table and grinned at me. The waiter came back with our brandy. "'Nother Dewar's," Rogers said. "No water, and for God's sake, this time keep the damn ice out of it."

"Look, Dr. Rogers," Karen said.

"Cam." Cozily.

"Cam. If you'd like to talk some other time—"

"Oh, no," he interrupted. "I'd rather talk now. I don't know anybody else here, and the evening's young. Want to run over the evidence I've gathered in this case, try to figure out who our practical joker is?"

"Tomorrow," Karen said firmly.

"Have you considered how easy it would be for Herman Miller to set up that landing site?" Rogers asked. "I'd like to get a good look into that barn of his, and all the sheds, too. But he's got those damn pigs—"

"Herm Miller!" Karen exclaimed. "That's ridiculous! He—" She clapped a hand over her mouth and gazed at me mournfully.

"He what?" prompted Rogers.

"He was so helpful," Karen said in a thin, tiny voice, as if she were trying to explain how her hand got stuck in the cookie jar.

"Just my point," Rogers crowed, and proceeded to elaborate. I sat shaking my head. How did the man do it? It wasn't just that he was tall, trim, and had the dark good looks of, say, a top male model. It wasn't that aura of energy barely contained. Plenty of other men had both and didn't take advantage of other people's politeness to insinuate themselves into their lives in this same outrageous way . . . or maybe they were just decent enough not to try. I felt my hands crooking into stiff, open curves ready to clamp around that muscular neck. Much good it would do me. *The guy probably has a black belt in karate,* I thought glumly.

Karen sat warming her snifter in hands so pale it looked as if the brandy would have more luck warming them. Her face

74

looked numb. I felt pretty numb myself, trapped. Oh, I could stand up, get ready to go, but then what? Rogers could just stick to his seat, blocking Karen, and then I'd have to stand around on one foot and then the other, until Rogers said something like "Look, if you've got to go to the john, we'll wait." And then I'd have to sit down again.

Which is precisely what happened when I tried it, except that Rogers said "little boys' room" instead of "john." People make themselves reputations as psychics with predictions no more accurate than that.

The waiter came over, face set for trouble, and *Karen* ordered another round! She might as well have kicked me in the stomach. "What do you mean, someone you shouldn't have seen?" she asked.

Wake up, J.J. How much had I missed, feeling sorry for myself?

"Did I say that?" Rogers cocked an eyebrow. His voice was getting louder. "P'r'aps I should've said, someone I was surprised to see. But that's really no concern of yours." A spasm of regret crossed Karen's face. I pricked up my ears.

"Oh," Rogers said, leaning back, booming. "Lotsa thin's goin' on 'roun' here you wouldn' know 'bout. Lotsa things. I might just stay for the weekend! Lotsa int'restin' stuff goin' on. . . . "

Someone in the booth behind me got up abruptly and my seat rocked gently. "Why don' we talk 'bout somethin' even more int'resting?" Rogers crooned to Karen, who was too tight against the wall to get any farther away. "Like you. Did you know you're a very attractive woman? Very, very 'tractive—"

"I've told her," I said, louder than I'd intended. Rogers glanced at me, clearly amused.

The drinks came as he opened his mouth for the next salvo. "Pardon me," the waiter said to him. "You aren't driving, are you, sir?"

"Why? Do I look drunk?"

"Uh, it's just that—"

"If it will help you soothe your putrid little conscience, I'm staying at the motel and I'm walking back," Rogers said, perfectly clearly but still too loud.

The farmboy-waiter set his square freckled jaw. "Anyway, the bartender said to tell you this is the last one."

"He told you to say that, did he?" Rogers eyed the kid. The eyebrow jerked. "And you always do what he says? Great big boy like you?"

One of the hands under the serving tray bunched into a fist, and that shoulder shifted backward and down. "Drop it, Cam," Karen said. She put her hand on his sleeve.

He patted it and caught it in a tight grasp. "Lady Kay, what do you say we ditch this creep husband of yours and go on back to the motel together? Hmm?"

My jaw sagged, and it was a split second before my own fists clenched. "Need any help here, sir?" the waiter asked me, with an undercurrent of enthusiasm for the help he was prepared to give.

"I think we'll be just fine as soon as Dr. Rogers is on his way," I said. "Alone."

"Aw, c'mon." Rogers grinned at me, a sloppy grin; he was even drunker than I'd thought. "She 'ready said no, what else d'you want?"

"You out of the booth."

"Okay, okay, okay," he said, patting each word into place. "C'n tell when I'm not wanted. No hard feelings, hey, J.J.? Not like some."

He's remembered again that I've got the car, I thought. He slid jerkily out of the booth, steadied himself with one hand on the table and the other on the stony-faced waiter, and headed fairly straight for the door. At the door he stopped, wobbled, and made a beeline for the bar.

"Now what?" Karen inquired of heaven.

Rogers dragged his wallet out of his back pocket and pulled out a couple of bills, flashing his wad of cash. The barkeep rang something up and took the bills. As he snapped change out of the register drawer, Rogers made a grandiose gesture with his left hand, tucked the wallet into his pocket, and drew his bearings on the exit.

The restaurant hostess opened one of the double doors for him. Rogers said something into her ear that made her put her free hand to her breastbone, and then he vanished into the night.

"Alone at last?"

"Alone at last," Karen affirmed, but her heart wasn't in it. She sipped a little brandy. "I wonder what he was talking about? Seeing somebody, I mean? He said it made everything quite clear, and now he knew what to do about it."

"I didn't hear that."

Her lips twitched in a half smile. "I'm not surprised. You looked like you were plotting murder."

"Not plotting," I said with dignity. "Fantasizing. There's a difference."

Karen's frown returned. "He'd been going on about Miller, something about his daughter, of all things."

"I didn't even know Herm had a daughter, but I can see Rogers being more interested in her than in him."

"Then he looked up at the bartender and said something like 'Speak of the devil,' and then that bit about everything being quite clear."

"I'm glad he thinks so. Clear as mud to me."

"Me, too. That's why I ordered more drinks—I was hoping he'd get sloshed enough to explain. I looked at the bar too, but all I could see was the same people who've been there all evening," she continued in a puzzled tone. "I wish I could remember his exact words, but I'm afraid I was concentrating so hard on wanting him to go away that I wasn't really listening."

The young waiter appeared again at the end of the table. "Everything okay here now?" he asked. The question was directed at Karen.

"Fine, thanks."

"Dr. Rogers hook up with his friend?"

"Friend?" Karen echoed.

"I don't think the guy could have any," I commented.

The waiter crooked one corner of his mouth as if he agreed, and said, "The guy who phoned. Said to just give him the word if the good doctor was walking, and he'd surprise him with a ride back. I guess because it's raining."

"Nice of him," I said. I sipped more brandy, and the waiter nodded at a raised hand and headed in that direction.

"Joe." Karen's voice was so strange that I stared at her. "Joe, I've got the most awful feeling. Why would anybody want to know if Cam was walking?"

"Alone at last?" I asked hopefully.

"Oh, you! No, I mean it. Somebody might be laying for him on his way back. He's been showing around all that money—"

"Serve him right if he got banged up a little and had his wallet cleaned out," I said.

"He hasn't been exactly ingratiating the past couple of days. What . . . what if somebody's planning something worse?" Karen gripped the edge of the table with both hands. "Joe, the guy's a bastard and I don't care if I never see him again, but we can't let him get *killed*."

"Why would anybody want to kill him?"

"Didn't you? Just now?"

That sat on the lovely glowing grain of the table for a minute and looked at me. "Oh, all right," I sighed, reaching for my wallet. I slid out of the booth and met the waiter on his way across the room, paid, collected Karen, and went out through the double doors. The hostess without pearls wished us a good evening.

The entrance was so much brighter than the bar that I blinked. The light under the entrance roof was still busy with insects that had escaped the few light frosts we'd had, and their shadows swooped around our feet as we walked down the four steps and out of the yellow circle of light. I blinked again, getting my bearings. The last of the daylight had drained over the horizon sometime during dinner. No moon or stars: clouds still covered the sky, and a rain like a heavy mist had begun to fall. It brought down with it a heavy odor of turned earth and turning leaves.

Small nameless creatures skittered through the darkness as we started down the path, and then, close overhead, we heard the chilling *hoo-hoo-hoo-hoo-hoo* of an owl. Karen jumped. I pulled her closer to my side.

"Let go," she said. "I want to find my flashlight." We walked

78

slowly along the path to the motel as she rummaged in her handbag. "Damn," she said. "Don't tell me it isn't here! I know I had it yesterday."

Ahead of us, maybe a third of the way along the path, Rogers was outlined against the lights of the motel sign, studiously putting one foot in front of the other. He wasn't weaving nearly as much as I'd expected; maybe the fresh air had done him some good. "Hey, Rogers," I yelled. He made a slashing motion with one silhouetted arm and stumbled on without replying. Karen gave up on the flashlight search and we walked faster.

We'd come within thirty feet of him when a blinding light stabbed out of the dark across the road, swept over us, and fastened on Rogers. He threw up a hand to shade his eyes. Three shots cracked the soft October air. Rogers jerked and fell.

"Too late!" Karen started to run.

I grabbed her. "Don't get shot yourself," I said. "Go back to the bar and get some help."

A motor roared on the other side of the road and a large vehicle, a van or a pickup—I couldn't tell which through the green haze the spotlight had left in my eyes—lurched onto the pavement and sped down the road past the motel. The taillights came on as I started for Rogers, brightening momentarily as the truck crossed the road repair near the motel and sped away.

"Here, here's the flashlight." Karen pressed something the size of a cigarette lighter into my hand. I fumbled with the switch, got a thin beam of light out of the thing, and ran for the dark heap on the path ahead.

Rogers opened his eyes and rolled them in my direction as I knelt beside him. They seemed larger than normal, and glassy, in the feeble light of Karen's flashlight. "I'm hit," he gasped.

"I know. Lie still."

"Douse the damn light," he said.

"I just want to see where you're hurt."

"Douse the damn light," he repeated with more vigor, struggling to grab it from me. "You want the gooks—" He coughed. As I thumbed the light off, I thought I saw blood on his lips. My left arm was beginning to throb: I remembered a sting when I'd heard the shots. *I've been hit myself,* I thought with an astonished wonder. *If I'd had my arm around Karen, still. . . .* The bullet had gone between us.

I felt a pain in my lower lip and realized I was biting it. "Medics," Rogers gasped. He sounded weaker.

"Coming. Lie still."

He whispered something that sounded like 'Chopper.' I put my ear close to his mouth, but he was finished talking. No sound but the ragged gurgle of his breath. I ripped open his shirt and risked stirring him up again with the light to locate the wound. Just above his right nipple, red froth around a jagged hole. I tried to remember what they'd told my Boy Scout troop, two-thirds of my life ago, about penetrating wounds of the chest, but all my mind dredged up for me was the far-off vision of my own smooth, half-formed hands steadying an auger to put holes in a thin white birch log to make a Christmas candle-holder, the blood-red candles in cellophane wrappers lying crisscross in a stack just at arm's reach.

Rogers coughed. I prayed that I was doing the right thing and clamped my hand over the ugly hole. A moment later, the beam of a good flashlight bobbled over us. Someone was running, coming to help. I pressed my hand tighter against Rogers's cool chest.

VIII

"GOSH, I NEVER thought," the freckled waiter from the Home Kitchen bar kept saying. "Gosh, I never thought," as regular as a heartbeat.

Maybe thirty people from the restaurant milled around on and off the road, and not a one of them had any better idea what to do for Rogers than I did—or if one did, he wasn't coming forward. Rogers had tried to turn on his side, the wounded side, and it looked like it couldn't hurt, so I'd helped him shift. I kept my hand clamped over the wound; my fingers were sticky with blood. The bullet didn't seem to have come out of his back. *Maybe it's still in there,* I thought. Whether that was good or bad, I didn't know.

Karen knelt beside me on the dirt path gabbling about relinings and trips to the reweaver, both designed to rescue my good sport coat from the rag bag. Maybe she just couldn't focus on my wounded arm; as for me, the pain made it harder and harder to try to pay any attention to Rogers.

He made no effort to talk, just gasped for breath. Something rattled as he breathed, and his face, shielded from the rain by a volunteer umbrella, ran sweat despite the cool October night. A long way away I heard a siren, as sweet as a lullaby, and cursed it for being so slow.

Something else occurred to me, out of the smell of wet leaves and blood. "Karen?"

She lifted her head out of her hands. "What?"

"Find somebody who looks like they could take charge and get him to keep people off the other side of the road, where that truck was parked."

"Truck?"

"The one that shot at us." *Trucks don't shoot people, people shoot people,* some ghost of a National Rifle Association voice-over said in my head. I gritted my teeth.

Karen was already moving, standing, searching among the faces in the crowd. She chose a shadow and spoke to it. A moment later the bartender came along the edge of the road, herding people onto the shoulder, his white apron reflecting the lights of the motel and the flashlight someone still trained on Rogers and me.

The siren had stopped while still some distance away—unneeded, I guess—so the red and blue lights flashing over us took me by surprise. Not an ambulance; two car doors slammed and a pair of well-worn, well-polished black boots came into my circle of vision. The owner of the boots put his hands on his blue-clad knees and bent over. The face that went with the boots was as young as the bar waiter's, equally fair and freckled, but had an air of competence that made me sigh with relief.

"What happened here?"

"Somebody shot him. Us." I raised my left elbow to display the two holes in my sport coat. The wound hadn't bled enough to come to the surface. "From a van or a pickup parked across the road."

"Where's the van now?"

"It took off."

"Straight west?"

"Straight west." The deputy straightened up, and one of the boots lifted and rotated as he turned to look across the road. He brought his face down again.

"You get a plate number?"

"No." Why not? I tried to picture the fleeing truck, saw only two red lights in my mind's eye, brightening just one brief instant as the truck crossed the road repair near the motel. "I don't think the plate light was lit."

Another, older and more genial deputy moved among the crowd, taking names and telling them to go back to the restaurant and stay there. Rogers's breathing had speeded up: shallow, choking respirations that came irregularly. "Can't we get some help for him?" I pleaded.

"It's coming. Volunteer firemen run the ambulance; they've

got to get to the firehouse first. Anybody else with you when this took place?"

"My wife." Where was she? A little thrill of panic skittered through me, delayed fear that plucked a string from my crotch to my breastbone. "Karen!" I bellowed.

"You don't need to yell." Sounding peevish. "I'm right behind you."

"Did you get a look at the license plate?" the deputy asked her. "Or a better look at the vehicle?"

"I didn't see it at all," Karen said. "I was looking in my purse for my little flashlight, and when the spotlight came on, I looked right into it and it blinded me."

"Spotlight." The deputy stood up. "Okay. You two stick around." The boots went away, casting stiff shadows over Rogers's face, and I realized that the flashlight had also gone away, that the light that bathed us now came from the police car. I couldn't look into it. A metallicized voice from the car acknowledged something; the deputy said something about a van or a pickup with no license-plate light.

"Won't he get pulled over anyway?" Karen asked me. "With no light on the plate?"

"Maybe." With a clarity approaching a vision, I saw in my mind's eye the van—I was almost sure, now, that it had been a van—skid to the side of the road, the driver jump out and run to the back of the idling truck, his hand reach out and peel the black plastic tape from the plate lamp and wad it into a ball that he threw to the floor of the van as he put it into gear and swung back onto the road. All in the space of, what? Thirty, forty-five seconds? Under a minute, for sure. And then the van picking up speed, the twin red lights now flanking a perfectly legal, well-lit license plate. That's what I'd have done, at least, and anything I can think of most other men can.

Too bad I'm not clairvoyant. Then I could have had the license number, too, and even if the van had made it to I-35—not unlikely, given the time it had taken to summon help—the state police could have pulled it in. But a good imagination isn't second sight, and as it was, the van could double back, get off the highway somewhere, and an "honest citizen" could go home and turn on the ten o'clock news to see if the story had made it to the Twin Cities or Rochester yet.

Another set of flashing lights skimmed over us. The ambulance had arrived, *sans* siren. "Hey," somebody yelled. "Out of the way!"

"Pull up on the other side" came the reply from a uniformed man standing in the road.

"What's going on?"

"We got a crime scene here. Get it over."

The ambulance roared forward, veered left, screeched, and backed along the gravel shoulder to come to rest just beyond the squad car. A paramedic materialized at my side. "What we got here?" he demanded.

"Chest wound. Under my hand."

"Good enough. You can let go." I lifted my hand and felt a gush of thick warm fluid between my fingers. The string of fear tightened again, so taut that I wondered for an instant if I'd ever make love again. My knees had stiffened with the long crouch and I staggered as I got to my feet.

"Whoa," somebody said. "You okay?"

"I'm hit too," I said. "My left arm." I lifted an exploring hand.

"Careful," Karen screeched. "Don't get blood on it too!"

"Christ, Karen, can't you think of anything but my damn coat?"

"Your arm's not bleeding," she said. "And the coat cost three hundred dollars."

I turned the sleeve toward the light and saw two neat small holes piercing the imported tweed. Nothing seemed to be oozing from my arm. "It hurts," I said, puzzled.

"Puncture wounds sometimes close up," the same somebody said. "Better get it looked at. Here." He held out a paper towel. I stared at it. "Wipe your hands," he said, in haste and disgust, and bent to help the others with Rogers. They bundled him into the ambulance with the rhythm of men used to pitching feed sacks. Two of the men hopped in after him, and another slammed the red doors. *Advanced Life Support Unit #1* they

84

announced in gold letters. Was there a unit number two? Probably not.

The ambulance rocked back onto the pavement and made a U-turn beyond the last of the blaze-orange cones the police had set out. What was left of the crowd backed away from the road as the red truck rocketed past with a single light touch of the siren. A stunned silence was left behind, into which the voices of the policemen dropped like pebbles. The half-dozen or so people who had stuck it out that long began to drift back to the dinners and drinks they'd left at the restaurant, arms still folded, talking little.

"What about me?" I asked in general.

Nobody answered. After a moment Karen said, "Let's walk back to the motel, if you feel up to it, and I'll drive you to the hospital. The clerk will know where it is. And then we'll go straight home."

"Home! Karen, we can't!"

"Joseph." Karen's voice was so calm I could scarcely breathe. "You promised."

"Karen, we're witnesses. We can't just cut out."

"You promised!" Fists clenched, almost shouting. "If there was any trouble, we'd go home, you *said* so, and I've put up with that man for two solid days, I've tried to be cheerful for your sake, and now I want to *go*—"

"Go where?" asked the older deputy.

Karen shut up.

"I've got a bullet wound in my arm," I said. "My wife's going to drive me to the hospital."

"No kidding?" the man said, as if I'd just breathlessly informed him that penguins can be found in Antarctica. "Let's have a look."

Two more police cars, one of them the maroon of the state patrol, had arrived; the sides of the road were lit with sweeps of crimson, but the spotlight that had been trained on Rogers and me had been shifted to the other side of the road. The deputy opened the rear door of the first car and waved me in, left the door hanging open, reached into the driver's side window to

85

turn on the dome light, then got in beside me. "Doesn't look like it bled any," he remarked.

I slid out of my jacket, astonished at how heavily the shoulder pad pressed on my arm as it slipped over my shirt. The shirt had the same two neat holes, closer together, but no blood; somewhat astonished, I stripped it off, too. Just at the edge of my T-shirt sleeve was a long, angry horizontal streak, the center of it raised in a thin blister perhaps two inches long.

"Aah, it's only a burn. You'll live," the deputy pronounced. "That guy a friend of yours?"

I stuck at "friend." "Um, say a colleague," I compromised. Even that seemed a bit much. "We came down from Minneapolis together to investigate that report of a UFO landing. He's been making himself pretty unpopular for the last couple of days." Good God! Had it been *yesterday morning* that I'd stood with my backside creased by my desktop, flipping over pages of printout and pointing out my notations to one of the engineers? My hands began to shake, and then my knees. I leaned my head against the back of the seat and felt my jaw trembling too.

"Hey, that thing in Herm Miller's field?" the deputy asked. "Pretty impressive, if you ask me. I hear it's radioactive."

"Not very." The shaking went through me again, like a hot chill.

"Herm's worried he won't be able to grow anything on it," the deputy said. "Or the dust'll get up in the summer and blow on his grandkids and give 'em cancer or turn 'em into monsters." The man chuckled. "I told him they're already monsters and nothing he can do about it."

"I don't see that amount of radioactivity causing many problems," I said. Somebody else's head was doing the talking, wasn't it? "It's only just above background level."

"Herm'll be glad to hear that. Those kids come every summer and school vacation. They're his daughter's kids by her first husband, you know? This'll give 'em something for show and tell, I bet."

"I bet," I said, without enthusiasm.

"That daughter of his. Must be nice to be able to dump your kids like that. First it was she needed the vacation, all the stress and strain of being a single mother, and now it's her and the new husband want some time to themselves. Spoiled rotten, the whole lot of them, if you ask me."

I hadn't.

"Not that I can't understand wanting to ball your wife without some kid hanging on your shirttail," the deputy added. It sounded like a conscious effort to be fair. "'Specially if it ain't your own kid."

The shaking subsided some; I finished pulling my own shirt over my burn and buttoned it. Didn't bother to tuck in the tail, but then my kid was over forty miles away and I was sitting in a police car. My tie, one of my favorites, was soaked in blood on the broad end. *One more thing to hold against Rogers,* I thought uncharitably.

"Well, look," the deputy continued. "I'm gonna drive on over to the hospital and see what we can find out from your, er, colleague as soon as he can talk, and I'd be glad to take you and the wife with. 'Sides, you're witnesses, somebody got to talk to you. Might as well be me. Lemme just check with the sheriff."

He got out of the car, leaving the other back door hanging open and a cool damp breeze blowing through. I shivered. When I picked up my jacket, I realized that it was thoroughly wet, but it was warmer than nothing, even if it smelled like a soggy sheep, so I put it on.

Karen got in beside me. The two back doors slammed. The young, freckled deputy got into the driver's seat and the older one, the genial guy who was so understanding about Herm Miller's daughter's second husband's problems, got into the passenger seat. The front doors slammed in unison.

We drove to the hospital. A nurse put a dressing on my burn and cautioned me not to take any needles to the blister, not even if I ran them through match flames first. The deputies asked me questions. They asked Karen questions. All four of us drank coffee out of a machine. The deputies smoked.

A little after one, the waiting ended. Cameron Rogers was dead.

Slowly, over the two-and-some hours we'd spent in that room

with its royal-blue carpet and soft-green plastic-upholstered chairs, it had dawned, first on Karen and then on me, how narrow our own escapes had been. Three shots for three people. Rogers had crumpled. I, Karen told me, had stumbled when the second bullet tore through my sleeve as I faced the van, and when I'd grabbed her, both of us had crouched. I didn't remember any of it.

"With the spotlight on Rogers, he couldn't have seen us too clearly," Karen thought aloud. "He'd have turned the light back if he could, so he must have had his hands full. . . . Joe, Cam was thirty feet ahead of us. Could a shot have gone that wide, at that distance?"

"Karen, what I know about guns you could put in a shell casing and not have enough pizzazz to go pop."

"Be serious." She pulled her nightgown over her head and plumped down into the motel room's single armchair with her hands clasped in her lap, and looked up at me. "That guy didn't want any witnesses, Joe. He missed Cam's heart by a couple of inches—that's good shooting. I wonder if he thinks he got us, too, or if he just decided he had to get out of there before he got caught?"

Sometimes Karen thinks too loud. "I don't know," I said, the words distorted by a yawn. "Kay, I've got to go to bed."

A few minutes later, to my surprise, our goodnight kiss lengthened and deepened. . . . I guess when you don't have a kid grabbing your shirttail, it's just natural to take advantage of the chance . . . or maybe it's just natural to celebrate when you've recently realized how lucky you are to be alive, and how quickly and unexpectedly that state can end.

IX

"JOEY'S NOT GETTING to be too much for you, is he?" Karen said into the telephone. "Oh, good. I don't know how long we'll be, but I'm assuming the sheriff will let us come home sometime today, since he didn't throw us in jail last night . . . as witnesses, of course!"

I dropped the edge of the curtain over a gray, misty morning and went into the bathroom for a shower, leaving Karen to sort things out with Lydia Eskew. I let the hot water drum on my thinning hair twice as long as I normally do, but it didn't wash the night before out of my mind; dreams of fleeing through dry grass taller than my head had wakened me twice and simmered still. The shower became a hot rain, and I wrenched it off. When I wiped the steam off the mirror and examined my face, I was startled to see that, other than a day's growth of beard and eyes bloodshot in the corners, it looked much as usual. I lathered up my jaw with the scrap of soap the motel provided and went at the beard with a disposable razor I'd picked up from their little shop the day before. The electric razor was out, maybe for good. Grisly associations, for one thing, and for another, I'd never get every trace of rabbit out of the thing.

Spiffy as I ever am, I left the bathroom and found Karen fully dressed and combing her hair. "He's an angel," she complained. "A *perfect* angel, no less! How come kids never behave as well for their parents as they do for other people?"

"You're asking me?" The skin beneath her eyes was almost black; even her cheeks looked hollow. I kissed her forehead and sat down to put on my shoes.

"You didn't get that dressing wet, did you?"

"No, the plastic worked." I rubbed my hands over a face that felt like cardboard. "I'd better call in, let them know I'll be an extra day," I said. "I hope just one extra day."

"Oh, that's right." Karen put her comb down. "Somebody from the sheriff's office called while you were in the shower. They want us to come sign statements."

I just grunted. I've had more experience with police and statements than any man should ever have. "When?"

"After breakfast will do."

I got things squared away with my boss, not without some tasteless teasing about the troubles I get myself into, and glanced at my watch. "Nine already," I commented. "How times flies when you're having fun."

"Fun for you, maybe."

"It was meant to be sarcastic."

"I should hope so." Tears started down Karen's cheeks; she glanced at me and turned her face away.

"Kay?"

She sobbed once. I tried to turn her, to take her into my arms, but she shook me off and put her hands over her face. "Kay," I pleaded. I walked around her and hugged her to me, her elbows pressing into my belly, and she began to cry harder. I rocked her, burrowing my nose into her lemony-scented hair, and felt my eyes squeeze shut against my own tears.

A few minutes later she said, "Joe, do you realize this is the third time you've been mixed up in a murder case because of CATCH? It scares me."

"Me, too," I confessed.

"Have you ever heard of it happening to anybody else?"

"It's got to." But to myself, I had to admit that I hadn't. Maybe midwestern UFOs are different from UFOs in New Hampshire or Pascagoula, Florida. More human, if less humane.

The telephone rang.

"More law enforcement," Karen predicted, backing off and reaching into her pocket for a crumpled Kleenex. I picked up the telephone.

"This is Cameron Rogers's head technician," said a somewhat querulous tenor voice. "I can't seem to get in touch with him and I wondered if you know where he is? It's important."

Maybe what I felt resembles what a window feels as the

90

stone goes through. I sat on the bed. "Uh, Dr. Rogers was shot last night," I said.

"Shot?" Small silence. "Could you tell me what hospital he's in? I really need to talk to him."

Why me? "I . . . I'm afraid you can't. He's dead."

Another silence. "I don't understand."

"Somebody took a shot at him last night," I repeated. "He died a couple of hours later."

"Oh." Short pause. Inanely: "He was hit, then?"

I swallowed. This was even harder than I'd thought it would be. "Yes, he was."

"I see." A longer pause. "What am I going to do?" the man wondered aloud. "I've got all these experiments running . . . three other technicians. . . . Have you notified anyone? Other than the police, I mean."

"No." That seemed too curt, so I added, "I don't know who should be notified."

"I guess . . . I guess I'd better go to the director of the lab." The man sounded a little brisker, a little more efficient. "Is there someone he could call, to get more details?"

I gave Rogers's head technician the sheriff's name and telephone number. "What's your name?" I asked.

"Mine?" For a moment, I wondered if I'd startled him out of remembering it. Or maybe nobody was very much interested in his name under other circumstances. "It's Anderson," he said. "John Anderson."

"Are you Bucky?"

"Yes, that's me. Why, was Cam talking about me?"

"Only to say you'd do a good job of running the lab in his absence," I said, trimming a little.

Pause again. "That's a first," Anderson remarked, and hung up.

I followed Karen out into a rain that drifted, instead of falling, out of the sky. She had her car keys out, unlocking the passenger side door. As I walked to the other side, she leaned across the seat and pulled up the lock button for me, something

Rogers hadn't bothered to do in the—only two days?—*day and a half* we'd been working together.

"This seems strange." Karen pulled down on the seatbelt and pushed it into the clasp beside her. "I feel as if I haven't sat here in weeks."

"I know what you mean." I put the key into the ignition and turned it. The act seemed spooky. I shook the feeling off and backed out of the space.

"Joe," Karen said, "isn't there a diner or something in Fox Prairie?"

"I don't remember one."

"Or even that McDonald's we had lunch at yesterday. Joe, let's go there for breakfast. I—the Home Kitchen—"

"Fine with me." I nosed out of the motel driveway and turned toward Fox Prairie, to pick up the country road that ran past Herm Miller's place. The police had set out bright orange cones around the place where Rogers had been shot, and a dark van with the crest of the sheriff's office decalled on the door was parked nearby. Two men in yellow slickers bent over the shoulder of the road where the other van had been parked the night before. I watched them in the mirror after I had passed, wondering what they were doing.

"Joe! Watch out!"

I looked at the road instead of the mirror and straightened out my drift into the other lane. "Sorry," I mumbled. I had the strange feeling that someone was sitting in the back seat. Probably because Karen's been there the past two days, I told myself. A SPEED LIMIT 30 sign, recently pocked by a shotgun, appeared on the right ahead, and I slowed for the short main street of Fox Prairie.

Right at the light, past the funny business that had started all this . . .

"Joe," Karen said abruptly, "do you ever believe in ghosts?"

"What kind of question is that? Of course I don't believe in ghosts."

"Never? Not even sometimes in the middle of the night?"

The sumac along the road was crimson, scarlet, carmine, bloody, already scattering leaves onto the pavement. A rabbit,

92

maybe the same one that had hopped out in front of us the day before yesterday, had been smashed and smeared into a blur of blood and fur in the opposite lane. Ahead, the road rose toward a meeting with the sky obscured by the misty rain that fed on itself, like fear. Over the top of the rise, hidden by brush, something had happened to make the ground radioactive, to cut up still another rabbit in a less explicable way, to leave olive-drab threads caught on wires and twigs—*Hold onto that, J.J.*—to flash lights in the eyes of Eagle Scouts. . . . "Maybe sometimes," I admitted grudgingly. "Never for long. Why?"

"I just wondered."

We were past the site, passing the end of the little dirt road. The blacktop with its fresh double yellow stripe rose out of the dip and stretched ahead, glossy with rain. Karen shook her head and settled into her jacket, the collar turned up.

A little later the speed limit began decreasing again, to lead us toward the Sausage McMuffin my tongue and stomach yearned for. "I can think of five people with decent motives for killing Rogers," Karen said. "That's if he set up the hoax himself."

"And if he didn't?"

"Maybe fewer," she said. "Maybe more."

Counting for myself, I thought, *She must be counting me,* and wondered what the sheriff really wanted.

A familiar blue van with an iridescent sunburst spread across the rear window glistened in the rain in the McDonald's lot. I pulled in next to it and set the brake.

"You want to eat with him?" Karen jerked her head toward the van as she got out.

"Not particularly. Might want to talk to him, though. I'd like to know where he went last night, after we left him."

"I bet a lot of people would." She smiled at me as I held the outer door of the restaurant for her and scrambled to push open the inside one.

"Hey, J.J.," Powell hailed us from a large booth. "Come on over."

Karen gave me a pale glance and started for the booth.

"Lookie here," Powell chortled as we came up. He made a

box of his fingers and placed them around a two-column item in the newspaper he'd spread out on the yellow table. "My story's on the back of the front section! How about that? Best I hoped for was to get it buried behind sports."

Karen slid into the opposite seat and I lowered myself into it after her. "Read it," Powell urged. "It's not bad. Didn't even run into overset."

"What's overset?" I took the section in self-defense as Powell thrust it at me.

"It wasn't too long," he translated. "So they put it all in. Too bad I only figured out that bit that was bothering me last night after the story was already in. All the guy would need is a portable radio that gets police bands, and he'd know when the deputies were coming. Then he could fold his tent and silently steal away. If he's good at camouflage, he's in business."

I skimmed to the end of the article, which seemed to be a reasonably concise summary of Saturday's events and what I'd thought of them. "You don't mention Rogers," I said.

Powell made a rude noise through his nose. "Him! What do I want with him?"

"I thought you two had made your peace," Karen said. "That's what he said last night. . . . "

Last night. I knew why Karen paused. The whole evening seemed half a lifetime ago until I closed my eyes; then it came back, vivid and *now*. "He said he'd offered to replace your tape and film and lens, and you'd accepted. He said everything was okay."

"Okay!" Powell flushed. "I don't know where that jackass thinks he gets off. For a lousy six bucks in film and tape and a lens I've got back anyway, he thinks I'll forget everything? I wouldn't forget one crummy second even if he crawls up and begs me for an interview! Oho, that's it! He remembered I'm a reporter—"

Karen glanced at me. "Jack," she interrupted. "He's dead."

"He's dead," Powell repeated in an absolutely flat voice. "What's that supposed to mean?"

"Somebody shot him last night, between the restaurant and

94

the motel. We were right behind him and saw it all. Didn't you know?"

"No." Powell took back the section of newspaper with his story in it; the corners of the pages fluttered as he folded it. "I was probably in my room, sending my story. Jeez. Wait'll my editor finds out. My head will roll."

"Sending your story?" Karen asked. "Do you call up and dictate, or what?"

"I let my TRS-80 do that," Powell said. "Look, I'd better get on this—you said you were right behind him?" The tape recorder magically appeared on the table. "Tell me."

"Not yet," I said. "First I want some breakfast. I just hope I can hold it down while I talk to you."

Powell rolled his eyes upward and grimaced in agony. "I got to get over to the sheriff's office, I . . . "

I left him listing what he had to do and ordered breakfast for two and an extra cup of coffee. Waiting for the tray to come, I glanced back at the booth. Powell was leaning eagerly toward my wife, his hands on hers, and she was slowly nodding her head.

I didn't mind a bit.

X

A HORN BLARED, and the blue van passed us at the edge of town doing seventy at a guess. Powell on his way to his story, trying to cut out any reporters who might already be covering it.

"He'll kill himself!" Karen exclaimed.

"You think that'll stop him?" I followed in his tire tracks for the few seconds it took for them to smooth over on the wet pavement, at a more sedate fifty miles an hour. Closest I've ever wanted to get to the Indy 500 is to pop a beer and catch a few laps on TV, and even those guys would think six or seven times before doing what Powell was doing. At a curve marked for thirty-five I slowed to thirty, half-expecting to see Powell's van upended in the ditch. But he'd apparently negotiated the bend successfully; no sign of the van, and a couple of crows were just settling back onto the shoulder of the highway. Karen sighed.

"Joe?" she said. "If somebody sends a story over the telephone line, doesn't that mean they have to be a certain place at a certain time?"

"Not really."

"Oh. Well, there goes that idea."

"You thought Powell might have an alibi?"

"Sort of." Karen sounded uncomfortable. She's not a woman who ordinarily thinks in accusatory patterns.

"Nah," I said. "With the TRS-80 he could set up his story and tell the computer to count to a million a few times before it sent it. Meanwhile he could be halfway to Kalamazoo if he wanted."

"Oh." The water on the road hissed under our tires and the rain misted the windshield between swipes of the wiper blades. Showers of dingy gold came out of a stand of elms ahead; I slowed down and looked for the blue van to have slipped on the slick wet leaves, but Powell had mastered this obstacle, too.

96

Karen stirred. "Joe? Wouldn't the telephone line have to be open while the computer was waiting to send the story, so the phone company could figure out when he left?"

"Uh-uh. He could program the machine to do the dialing, too. Nobody would know the difference."

Karen sighed again, noisily. "So much for my detective powers."

Speed-limit signs appeared ahead. The county seat was a bigger town, where roughly twenty-five hundred people lived, and served as the shopping center for the smaller towns nearby. It showed. For the first time since coming south, we were slowed by traffic, even had to stop once outside a yellow brick school building where cut-paper pumpkins and ghosts had been taped to the windows.

"Oh, dear," Karen exclaimed. "I haven't figured out how to turn Joey into a Viking yet."

"Why does he have to be a Viking?"

"For Halloween, silly."

A woman carrying a red umbrella hurried across the street in front of us while I tried to imagine my small-boned, dark-haired son as either a rampant Norseman or a football player. "I hope this is over by Halloween," I allowed to escape.

"Oh, Joe! It's got to be!"

I glanced at Karen's profile. She stared straight ahead, her lips so tight they had disappeared, her fists working in her lap. "Don't worry," I soothed. "I'm sure—"

"You don't know any more about it than I do," she flared. "So don't give me that. Honestly, Joe, when we get out of this one, I swear—"

"Okay, okay," I said, before she could finish. "Just calm down. We'll take it a step at a time."

We crossed a side street into a block lined with prairie-style houses that had been converted into stores by enlarging the windows and enclosing the porches, and then another, into a block of the familiar red brick buildings that formed the heart of every town in the area. I spotted a self-service gas station and pulled up to the pumps to fill up the wagon. Karen stayed in the car while I got out into the rain and pumped the gas. Done, I sorted out the glass door of the station from the steamy windows plastered with notices about church socials and local elections and went in. "Can you tell me where the sheriff's office is?" I asked the kid behind the counter as I paid for the gas.

"Sure." He gave me directions suitable for any moron, leaned on the top of the cash register and held onto my change while he repeated them and collected my nods at the end of each part, then wished me a nice day.

"Thanks," I said. Despite his good wishes, the rain was heavier than when I'd entered his warm, dry lair. A splot of water from the edge of the roof made a bull's-eye on the back of my neck as I dashed for the car.

Karen clicked the glove compartment closed on the notebook we use to keep track of our gasoline as I got into driver's seat. "Well," she sighed. "Here goes."

I'd thought we'd at least see the sheriff. No such luck. We produced our driver's licenses for the inspection of a middle-aged clerk, who pushed her glasses down her nose to look over them at us and agreed that we seemed to be who we claimed to be. Maybe. She hunted through some papers on a desk and came up with some typed pages for us to sign. "Be sure to read them first," she said, bored. "Sign every page. If you want to make a change, cross out what's wrong and write your correction in and initial that. Then bring everything back to me and I'll notarize it."

"How's the investigation going?" I asked.

"I'm not at liberty to say," she replied in the same bored voice.

I'd just finished reading over my statement and signing all the pages when the door to an inner office opened and Powell popped out, giving effusive thanks to an older man in a blue pin-stripe suit.

"Hey, J.J.!" he greeted me, and turned back to the man. "This is the guy I was telling you about, Sheriff. He can tell you all about the setup in Miller's field." Powell clapped me on the shoulder. "Gotta run and find a phone," he said joyfully. "Can you beat it? I'm the only one here besides the stringer! See you."

"What's a stringer?" I asked, but the outer office door was already whispering shut on its brass pneumatic elbow, and Powell's running footsteps sounded in the corridor.

"It's somebody who works part-time for a newspaper," the sheriff supplied. "Whenever there's a story, he sends it in. I think they call them that because they spend so much time fishing for good stories." At my blank look, he sighed. "Little joke there. 'Account of a stringer's what you keep your fish on once they're caught."

"Oh." I tried a laugh, but it came out a little odd. "Sorry, I'm not a fisherman."

"In Minnesota? You're missing a lot that way, son, let me tell you."

Somehow I had been maneuvered into the inner office, and this tall, gray-haired man was just shutting the door. As he shook my hand and said his name, I remembered that one of the offices that turns up on my ballot every so often is that of sheriff. Politically speaking, he was obviously a winner.

"Powell's been telling me about this thing over on Herm Miller's field," he said. Squeezing past a gold-fringed American flag that drooped morosely in a corner, he sat down at his desk and flopped a hand at a chair for me. The polished wooden seat was still warm, a faintly unpleasant surprise. "I'd like to hear about it from you, as the remaining expert," he continued. "What I read in the paper isn't always what I see in my courthouse. I like to check up on these reporters whenever I can."

"Did you see this morning's Minneapolis paper?" I asked.

"It's in there, is it?"

"The basics. And pretty accurate."

The sheriff leaned back in his chair and pressed his fingertips together, the picture of a man prepared to be reasonable. A carefully presented picture, I was sure. "I'd still like to hear this out of your own mouth," he said. "Might have some bearing on this case that our friend Mr. Powell didn't see."

Gently, deviously, the man teased out of me everything that

had happened between Sunday morning, when Ed Gustafson called, and Tuesday night, when the deputies had delivered Karen and me to the motel. He sat nodding quietly for a few minutes after my last answer had run down.

"What do you think of Powell?" he asked suddenly, sitting forward with a clank of his chair.

"I—I hardly know the guy," I said, startled. "I talked to him once last summer for a story for his paper, and that was the only time I'd seen him before he turned up here."

"How come he turned up?"

I had to think about that. "I don't know. I can't remember. . . . I thought he said somebody from your office called the paper, but you'd know about that . . . or, wait. Did he say Ed Gustafson called him? I can't be sure."

"I can't see one damn reason why Ed should call in the city papers, and a bunch why he shouldn't." The man sucked his lower lip in thoughtfully. "Must have been the stringer."

"This morning, though, Powell seemed surprised to hear that Rogers had been killed," I commented, following what I thought might be his train of thought.

"Powell? How'd he find out?"

With the sheriff's help I described my breakfast, down to Powell's fourth cup of coffee.

"That's where you were, then," he mused. A silence stretched out, sharpened by voices in the outer office, the rattle of a typewriter on the other side of the wall, a ringing telephone.

"Jamison, I need a little help here," he said. "I know all these other guys you've mentioned from way back. We were all in school together. The one I don't know is Powell."

"You don't know me, either," I pointed out.

"Aah, you're all right," he said, with a dismissive jerk of his head. "Your wife could've shot you, to make things look good—no problem there. But no way you could've shot that guy and got rid of the rifle in the time you had. I got a good timetable from the folks in the bar, and there's no sign of the thing in your room or your car." He grinned. "Or in the ditch."

I was startled, but that didn't stop my curiosity. "It was a rifle, then?" I asked.

"Rimfire .22."

I nodded, just as if he'd told me something I understood.

"That's what made it so bad," the sheriff explained. "A bigger slug might've gone right through, but this one was too light. Bounced off his rib cage and sliced up his lungs and his spleen." He noticed my wince and added, "Sorry. Forgot the guy was a buddy of yours."

"Not a buddy," I said. "We were just working together on this one case."

He grinned again, showing two improbably neat rows of white teeth. "So I heard."

"Not that that means I don't want you to catch whoever shot him," I said. "The rifle should narrow things down some, shouldn't it?"

"You got to be kidding." The sheriff leaned back in his chair and let it swivel gently. "You don't hunt, either, I take it. Every other guy in the county's got a .22 rifle, so no, it's not narrowed down much." He looked at his watch. "Now, I've got some appointments I have to take care of, but tell you what. I'll meet you at Herm Miller's place this afternoon, oh, say, three-thirty. I want a guided tour over that ground. You still got that rabbit?"

My stomach lurched. "Not me. Might be in Rogers's cooler."

"Oh, yeah, with his germs and stuff. That's impounded; I'll get it examined. What's the name of the guy with the soil samples?"

I told him, told him to check with Ed Gustafson on the spelling. A moment later, without quite realizing how, I found myself standing again in the outer office, with Karen holding my hand and staring into my face.

By early afternoon, the clouds had begun to break up, and an occasional smudge of sunlight drifted across fields blackened by the rain. Behind the motel some small bird greeted this development with a chirruping song I vaguely recognized.

"Goldfinch," Karen said. "Let's take a walk, Joe. I can't just sit around in this room waiting. I'll go nuts."

So that was what we did, took a long walk into the town of Fox Prairie to discover that there was a small bar around the corner from the main street after all, where we could get thick roast-beef sandwiches on chunks of French bread accompanied by a slice of garlic pickle that brought tears to my eyes, and a "bottomless" cup of strong coffee. Midafternoon was a slow time. The proprietress, a lanky woman whose blond-stained gray hair had been slicked into a thin braid and wound twice around her head, was happy to lean on the bar and chat with us across the six feet of scuffed wood floor between it and the booth we were sitting in.

She, too, had heard that the site where the saucer had supposedly landed was radioactive. I told her I thought Herm Miller had little to worry about.

"That's a relief." She straightened up with her hands on the small of her back. "Herm's worried about what he can grow there, and those grandkids of his, he drags 'em around with him all summer long—riding the tractor, feeding the hogs, any old thing he might do. You folks need more coffee in that pot?"

"No thanks." My hands were beginning to shake from all the coffee I had drunk as it was.

"Dumb kid of his," the woman sniffed. "Had a perfectly good husband with a perfectly good job up in the cities, nice to her and the kids, everything a woman might want—I expect so, anyway, with three kids in four years—and she goes and runs off with some dago."

"Oh, really?" Karen didn't sound the least bit interested, but the woman chattered on.

"Sensible enough to get married again, though," she allowed. "Even if it wasn't to the guy she run off with."

Old story. I made a mental note not to ask Herm Miller about his daughter if the chance arose.

"Now, Herm's son, that's a different matter," the woman opined. "Went up to the university, got himself a degree, and he's down in Texas working for NASA. 'Course, Herm'd like the farm to stay in the family like it has the last hundred years and more, and if he can just hang on long enough, that oldest grandson might take it over. He's only just turned eleven now, 'course."

Karen half-smiled.

102

"Good solid kid, though some might wonder about him. Likes to pull a prank now and then, but what red-blooded American boy doesn't?" She dropped her eyelids half over her blue eyes and smiled slowly. "And he's in school fifty miles from here this time of year, 'course."

Ah. So that was it. We were not to think the boy had anything to do with what was possibly a UFO hoax. "Of course," I said.

"Herm does dote on that boy. Bought him a good cow just last weekend. Two thousand dollars, how's that for a birthday present? Herm'll keep it for him, 'course."

Karen smiled.

Eyes open, our hostess stretched her back again. "Well, I do hope you get that whole thing settled pretty soon. Quite a hoo-hah in here last night, what with Clem Jacobson telling what he saw—gets better every time I hear it, 'course, but that's Clem for you—and a couple of his neighbors going on about how he was fooled. Though I can't deny it's nice to have something to talk about besides the high school." For a moment, she looked a trifle wan. "You folks need more coffee?" she asked again.

"No thanks," I said. "In fact, we ought to be going. Nice talking to you."

"You ever down this way again, drop in," she said, looking wistfully after us. Two women standing on the corner nudged one another as we stepped out onto the street. Celebrities already.

"I don't think I'll come along when you go to meet the sheriff," Karen said. She yawned. "I'll just take a nap, if that's okay with you."

"Sure." I could stand a nap myself, I thought, watching Karen detour around a struggling earthworm washed out of its burrow by the morning's rain. But meeting the sheriff wasn't quite the amiable arrangement he'd made it seem. It was an order, nicely buttered over but an order nonetheless, and I had the distinct impression that needing a nap wouldn't be an adequate excuse for not showing up.

*   *   *

By three-thirty the clouds had become a flock of newly washed sheep scattered over the sky, and a tentative sunlight touched the ridges left by plows as if it were too shy to penetrate the furrows. I was a couple of minutes late, sure that the sheriff would have made it a point to be early, and therefore puzzled as I came over the top of the hill to see no car pulled to the side of the road. Then I noticed a car, white with the broad brown stripe of the sheriff's office, in Miller's yard. I slowed for the sharp right into the drive.

The rain had left a thin slick of mud that rattled against the underbody of the station wagon as I drove toward the white farmhouse. The door of the sheriff's car swung open, and he got out and motioned to me to pull over onto a grassy space beside the drive. He'd changed out of his pinstripe suit into a plaid wool shirt and twill slacks that whistled one leg against the other as he strode toward me.

"Exactly where is it?" he asked through my rolled-down window.

"Little bit past the end of the drive."

"South?" When I nodded, he said, "We'll take your car. Just turn around in the yard; Herm knows we're here and he won't mind."

He got in and I made the circuit I had two days before, skidding a little in the muddy ruts, and the short drive to the landing site. The sheriff looked at my joggers with disapproval. "You're gonna get good and wet. Where's your boots?"

"I'll be okay."

He grunted. "Not a farmer, either, I can see that," he said, and climbed out of the wagon.

Whatever else I wasn't, I'd been right about the rain: it had changed things. Even the smell of the place was different; damp earth and the pungent scent of wet, decaying vegetation. The weeds along the road were beaten down in different patterns, and as we tramped toward the edge of the field I could see little sign that four or five people had been walking around in the brush. The three holes where the "landing feet" had made their impressions remained, but the sheen where the earth had been crushed was gone, and it would take an educated eye indeed to

104

see the difference between the circle and the rest of the field. I pointed out to the sheriff where it had been. He stuck his hands in his back pockets, working his jaw.

"And those little things are where the whatsit is supposed to've walked out of its saucer and back, huh?" he asked.

The oval depressions were almost indistinguishable from the ground around them, after our messing them up with plaster and a night and a morning of rain. The sheriff had an impressive eye for detail. "Yes," I said. "We've got casts of them."

"You told me," he reminded me. "I sent a deputy to pick 'em up from Rogers's room this morning."

"He got the other stuff, too, then?"

"Uh-huh. Show me where this rabbit was."

I led him to the spot, where he scraped the toe of his boot over the torn empty tube of matted grass left where Rogers had picked up the twig. His eyes flicked toward me, like the bob of a pocket gopher out of and into its hole. "You could have told me the damn thing was hot."

"Hot?" Nobody had put any ice in the cooler, of course, not after Rogers was shot. "It must have smelled to high heaven."

"That, too, but that's nothing. I mean radioactive."

"The *rabbit* was radioactive?"

"That's what I said."

I heard a distant cawing and looked up to see a crow fly south high over the field, chased by a pair of dots I could tell were blackbirds only by what they were doing. The radioactivity, of the circle and now of the slaughtered rabbit, seemed to harass me the way blackbirds do crows. "I don't see how that could be," I said.

"Well, two or three weeks, when the lab gets done with it, maybe we'll know," the sheriff said. "Let's have a look at that dirt road."

We walked down to the road, although the sheriff first made for the station wagon; nobody walks in the country but kids. The tracks of four turns by a four-wheeled vehicle and one by a two-wheeler were even less distinct than they had been the afternoon before. The sheriff's hands went again into his back pockets. Maybe that's where he keeps his trade secrets. His jaw worked as he gazed at the tracks.

"What's the wheelbase on that wagon of yours?" he asked.

"Hell, I don't remember."

"Shorter than the other vehicle, and the wheels aren't quite as far apart," he said. "You got a picture of these?"

"No."

"Too bad. Would've been nice to have them a little fresher. Well, for the sake of completeness I guess we'd better see what we can get. I'm not betting it's gonna mean anything to us, though." We started back for the station wagon along the edge of the blacktop. "What kind of car did Rogers drive, do you know?" he asked.

"Little two-seater, a Triumph. That's why we came down together, he couldn't begin to fit all his equipment in his own car."

"Huh."

We had reached my car. The sheriff stood beside it a moment with his hand on the door handle, looking around, at the site and at the sky. Then he got in, quickly, and slammed the door. I started the engine and made a U-turn in the road, to avoid marking up the gravel road any more than it had been already.

"I wonder if Rogers didn't do this himself, shoes or no shoes," the sheriff mused. "Wouldn't be hard to get somebody to help out. He had plenty of cash to spread around. Was that print a boot or a shoe?"

"That we found yesterday?" The print hadn't been all that clear, but you'd think the heavy stitching around the edge of a boot sole would show up anyway. "Hard to say," I decided finally, as I turned left into Miller's drive and bumped and slid along to pull up behind the official car. Miller appeared briefly in a shaft of sunlight between two buildings, seeming not to notice his visitors.

The sheriff reached out and turned off the ignition. He settled back comfortably against the seat and folded his arms. "See, if I come out here and try to figure out who did this"—he jerked his head toward the field to our left—"I'm saying I

106

believe I'm looking for a hunter, and that's not too likely. I think I'm looking for a plain killer."

"I don't get you."

He rolled down his window and hung his right elbow over the edge of it and looked at his hands as if they could tell him something. "Let me see how to put this," he said. "A hunter—I mean a real hunter, not one of these jerks comes out on a weekend and blasts up everybody's fence lines with a shotgun he borrowed from his brother-in-law first time last Thursday—a real hunter has to know what he's hunting. Not just what animal. I mean *know* it, so he can walk in its place, think with its brain, smell with its nose . . . like Herm's cat over there, see her?"

The cat I'd seen festooned on a step the first day down here was now crouched about twenty feet away in the thinning shade of the elms, intent upon something I couldn't see.

"See how she's got her belly down, making herself real small? Against those leaves, if you're short-sighted like maybe a vole, you couldn't hardly see her. She'll watch like that for at least a couple of minutes before she decides if it's worth making a grab, just watching. . . . " He stopped talking, but he had me watching the cat as if mesmerized. After a minute or two she sat up and elaborately licked her right front paw.

"Now, there!" I jumped at the sheriff's voice. "Whatever she was watching was on to her, and she knew it. So she'll let it go, for now, not waste any energy on it. Now, if that cat were a killer, instead of a hunter, you'd see her rush up and pounce, and whatever it is would be on its way, laughing its head off. Unless she just plain had some dumb luck; everybody's entitled to a little of that now and then. Now, if this saucer hoax is any part to the murder I'm looking at, then I'm looking for a hunter. Somebody who set up a trap and sucked Rogers into it, like you read about those elephant hunts where they dig a pit in a trail and cover it up and wait . . . or even like some kid sets up a trap line, for that matter. The kid *knows* where a raccoon's likely to travel—at least, he'd better if he wants to make any money—same as those guys in India *know* the elephant's gonna walk over that trail. And who's gonna *know* Rogers will come down here to investigate this UFO?"

"Me, for one."

The sheriff laughed and stretched. "You, you're no hunter. You're not even a killer, not like this one."

I thought of my stiffened hands in the bar, not half an hour before Rogers was shot. "I'm not so sure."

"Oh, sure, somebody pushes you into a corner, you might go off your head, like anybody can," he allowed. "But by the time you went home and picked up your rifle and got it loaded, let alone made a phone call to make sure your guy's still available, like that guy did last night, you'd have cooled off enough to see you didn't really want to do that."

"Comforting to have someone show such faith in my good sense," I said dryly.

He grinned. "Aah, I'm only telling you something's true of ninety percent of the populace. Besides, you didn't have a rifle and you were sitting in the bar when the call came in. Now, this guy I'm looking for is enough of a hunter that he knows to go get his gun and lay for the guy he wants where he's likely to travel, and he even cares enough to throw a light on him, make sure he's got the right guy, but I don't connect that with this UFO hoax. That's just too elaborate, see? And I'll tell you, what I'm hearing about this friend, uh, colleague of yours."

The genial deputy sure made complete reports.

· "He was one of these characters who's never happy unless he's got everybody around him all riled up. Half a dozen people could have had a reason to be sitting in that van or whatever it was." He flicked a glance at me between narrowed lids. "You sure you can't remember what it was?"

I thought about it. "Sorry. The spotlight blinded me, and the angle was wrong. I *think* it was a van, that's the best I can do."

"Sure you're not just casting a little doubt because your pal Jackson Powell's got a van?"

Well, was it? I'm a sucker for underdogs, as I should know by now. "He's not my pal," I said. "Just a guy who interviewed me for his newspaper once." And that reminded me. "Which reminds me, literally anybody could have known Rogers would investi-

108

gate this UFO. He said in the *Tribune,* last summer, he'd take on any case that looked like this."

"Huh." The sheriff thought this over for a moment, but when he spoke again he was back to Powell. "You know he had a practically new .22 Winchester Magnum Rimfire in that van?"

The cat had located another potential victim, or maybe the same one grown overconfident and careless. Even her lashing tail stilled as she crept over the fallen elm leaves in almost perfect silence. I could feel surprise, a numbness somewhere behind my face, at what the sheriff had said, but it still hadn't quite hit me. "I didn't know that," I said, still watching the cat.

"'Course, you can get them from J. C. Penney, so they're not exactly scarce, and he's got a valid small-game license, and the magazine's full, or was before we test-fired it." Big sigh. "It'll be at least a week before I hear anything on that. So I don't have enough to pull him in, not yet."

The cat took another flowing step. That would be how the Indians learned to travel so silently, by watching the cougar stalk her prey.

"Then there's Ed Gustafson, and Herm here, and that dingaling over at the school, Stemmermann. Hunters, every one of 'em. Been out with them all one time or another, myself. But any reasons they've got for hunting Rogers are all come up in the last couple days, so far as I can figure out. So, could be one of them set this up"—he nodded toward the sliver of sumac that showed over the top of the small rise in Miller's field that hid the landing site—"but not likely the same one that did the shooting. Too risky. So, far as I'm concerned you can poke at this all you want. I don't think you'll find any surprises, but if you do, give a holler, okay? Well, here's Herm."

A battered blue pickup jolted from behind the barn and stopped. I watched it for a moment, until a yellow blur caught my eye.

The cat had her mouse. The thing squeaked for mercy as she tossed it gracefully from paw to paw. No mercy there. Beside me, the sheriff levered himself out of the front seat of my car as smoothly as any cat, and waved at Miller as the truck's gears ground and it moved closer.

*   *   *

Two hours later, Karen and I had packed the station wagon and were speeding north along I-35, hoping to get home before Joey's bedtime. Left behind was the puzzle of Cameron Rogers's murder; that was for the sheriff to solve. And until he did, and our testimony was needed at a trial, I'd have nothing more to do with it. *My* puzzle was the UFO hoax, pure and simple, and that would be the only connection I'd have with events in Fox Prairie for a while.

At least, that's what I thought. What I'd seen happen to a mouse that afternoon should have reminded me of a famous quote about best-laid plans, one even an engineer would recognize.

XI

WE HAD TO park in the driveway. Rogers's cloth-topped Triumph had been locked in our garage for safe-keeping, a problem I'd have to deal with soon. A distraction was provided instantly; the phone was ringing when I shoved my key into the front-door lock. It stopped, as telephones usually do, an instant before I got to the kitchen and laid a hand on it. Faintly relieved, I took the suitcase from Karen and carried it into the bedroom, where the other extension gave a clipped chirp as if clearing its throat, and the phones started to ring again.

"I'm sorry," I said to the pleasant representative of the local press who proved to be on the other end of the line. "I'm a witness in the case, and I've promised not to discuss it with anyone." A bald-faced lie, but it sounded good, and might buy some peace.

"Who was that?" Karen asked when I went back to the kitchen. I told her. "I might have known," she sighed. "Joe, Lydia Eskew just came over to invite us to supper—I said I'd ask you, but I think we'd better take her up on it, don't you?"

"Good Lord," I said. "I hope she hasn't—"

"I'm sure she has," Karen interrupted. "So I really think we'd better help her eat it all, or the poor dear will have leftovers for weeks. And that freezer of hers isn't very big."

The phone was ringing as I pulled the door to behind me. I twisted the key in the lock and set off with Karen to join my son at Mrs. Eskew's banquet.

When the three of us came back, fed to the point of actual, groaning pain, I unhooked the kitchen phone from the wall plate and pulled the plug on the one in the bedroom. By quarter to ten we had even managed to salt Joey away in his bed. Serenity reigned.

For maybe ten minutes.

The rata-tat-tat of our door knocker sounded too resolute to believe that the person using it would go away, so I put my magazine down and heaved myself out of the chair I'd just settled into and went to the door.

"Hi," I said. "What do you want, another interview?"

Jackson Powell shrugged, his fair head to one side, and grinned sheepishly. "Not exactly. I hear you can't talk, anyway."

"Word gets around," I said, startled but not about to set him straight. "What do you want?"

"Help."

"From me?"

"From you. I think you're the only one who can help me." His cherub-face was shadowed by the porch light, the corrugations of his forehead thrown into sharp relief; he was wearing the same shabby corduroy jacket and the tear in the sleeve still gaped open. Pushover, soft touch, sucker for appeals to my vanity, whatever I am, I resisted for all of three seconds.

"You'd better come in."

He bobbed his head in a diffident way I hadn't seen from him before and stepped over the threshold. A faint smell of liquor came with him. "Karen," I called, "we've got company."

"I hate to bother you when you only just got home," Powell mumbled to Karen. "I've got a problem, though, a bad one, and I think maybe J.J. can help me out."

"I was just making some coffee," she said. "Decaf." Her voice was a little colder than the words, but she managed a smile. "Come on into the kitchen."

"I'm under suspicion," Powell announced, seated at the table circling a mug of milky coffee with both hands. "That jerk sheriff thinks I shot Rogers."

"Did you?" Karen asked.

Powell's mouth fell open. "Me?" After a moment in which no one said anything, he said, "I don't shoot anything."

"Nothing?" I asked.

"I have trouble squashing centipedes," he declared.

"What about the rifle in your van?" I asked. "What about your small-game license?"

112

Powell took a deep breath through his nose and let it out slowly. "It's that damn fool editor of mine," he said. "Thought it would be good sympathetic coloration on a story I did a couple of weeks ago—you know, people would open up a little better if they thought I hunted, too, so maybe I'd understand about selling a little illegal pheasant meat. Anyway, I took out the license, and I borrowed the gun from my next-door neighbor, and I never got around to giving it back before he took off for a week in Las Vegas."

"What's a rifle like that cost?" I wondered aloud.

"I got no idea. Hundred bucks, maybe."

Karen got up and went into the family room without saying anything. I heard the faint *ping* of the door catch of the couch-side table, the one she calls her miscellany cupboard.

"Now the sheriff's got my neighbor's gun impounded and he's coming back from vacation Friday, and bet you anything he'll want to use it this weekend," Powell complained. "He's not going to be happy to hear I haven't got it. And to top everything off, the damn thing was never out of its case the whole time, so it might as well have stayed in his closet."

"With the tax, I figure roughly two hundred and seventy-five dollars," Karen reported, crossing the kitchen to sit down again. She looked at Powell, waiting for a reaction.

"For the gun?" He whistled. "How do you figure that?"

"I looked it up in the Penney's catalog."

"Christ, and the thing's just been laying around the back of my van for two weeks!"

"Loaded," I added.

Powell's mouth fell open again, not quite so far, and his pale complexion turned pasty. "Loaded?" He swallowed. "You, uh, mean Mike gave me the thing *loaded?*"

"It's your story, not mine."

Powell stared at the table in front of him for several seconds, his face totally blank. "Well," he said finally. "Thanks for the coffee, anyway. I was going to say, help me get off this hook and I'll help you figure out how that hoax was done, but after a story like that I guess you won't even let me past your front door again."

"Trade help?" Karen tilted her head. "That's a good idea."

Both of us stared at her. "You mean you'd trust me?" Powell asked. "Are you crazy?"

"No to both. But I don't see how you could hurt, unless you did the hoax yourself, and you can probably account for where you were last Saturday night."

"Covering a fire . . . " The words jerked out as if he had thought them a thousand times.

"And you could have thought up a better story than that, if the gun's really yours. Do you have that hunting license with you?"

"Sure." Powell got out his wallet, extracted the license, and dropped it into Karen's outstretched hand.

"Issued thirteen days ago," she said, displaying it to me before she returned it to Powell. "And small-game season starts in the middle of September—I remember noticing that in the paper, because I thought we'd have to be careful if we went out for a day in the country. If you were really a hunter, you'd have taken the license out sooner."

Powell hesitated. "I guess it's lucky I never had to show it, then."

"Probably." Karen smiled a dry little smile. "One other piece of luck—I don't know much about hunting, but I do know you don't hunt birds with a rifle."

Powell groaned. "No wonder I never got near that story."

Karen got up and brought the coffeepot back to the table. "How do you think you can help us?" she asked.

Us. I liked that word, us.

"I have this, for starters." Powell pulled his newspaper ID out of his wallet and laid it on the table next to the hunting license. "Sometimes it opens doors, if it doesn't lock them. And I have the run of the newspaper's library, any time at all, which might help. A lot of connections."

And how could we help him? "You're better at sorting stuff out than I am. Faster. I've seen that already, even before I got to feeling panicky. And you know these people, some of them. I don't. . . . "

*　　*　　*

114

Karen turned to me as I latched the front door behind Jackson Powell. "It must be catching." She sounded bewildered. "How could I? After the last three days? I'm as bad as you are."

"You never could resist a puzzle."

"In the back of *Harper's* or the *Atlantic,* maybe." She drew a deep breath, with a wobble at the top of it, and sighed. "You think that's it? I think maybe I'm a little crazy, like Powell said."

"Not you," I assured her. "You really think that story he told us about the rifle is true?"

She shrugged. "He may be guile layered upon guile, for all I know, but you're right, I can't stand not knowing every detail of how that hoax was done. Because it seemed so *plausible* . . . the hoax, I mean. So if he can help figure it out, I'll take it. Won't you? Now that we're home again? With a little distance between us and . . . that?"

"Sure." I hugged her, one arm, sideways, as we walked through the house. "But for now, let's see if we can catch the end of the news and weather and go to bed." We were in the family room by then, and Karen flicked on the TV.

I stared at it in disbelief. Instead of a supergroomed weatherman reading from a teleprompter, a few small men stood like gems on a brilliant green setting. The camera zeroed in on one of them, and a baseball popped into his glove. "Two away," said the announcer. With the distractions of Fox Prairie over the past three days, I hadn't even realized I was missing the World Series!

" . . . do tomorrow?" Karen asked.

"Tomorrow? You'll get Joey off to school and spend some time writing, and I'll go to work. One of us had better find out what to do about Rogers's car. It can't stay where it is."

"Me, I guess," Karen sighed. "But what about this hoax?"

"Saturday, I'll give Powell a call and we can see what's up. Simple as that." I sat down in front of the TV, vowing not to miss one more minute of the action.

Which goes to show how little I really knew about Jackson Powell.

In the late sixties and early seventies, theoretical physicists were a glut on the job market. A lot of them, clutching degrees still warm from the college president's hand, did an about-face and went back to school for a few courses in computer science, the better to put bread in their mouths and bread in their pockets. We had a few of these displaced aristocrats working at the plant, and Thursday morning I collared one of them and took him to lunch. During the course of stuffing my face, I pocketed several paper napkins adorned with blotted inky diagrams, and went back to work wondering how five slices of pepperoni pizza that were mostly empty space (as my tame physicist had assured me they were) could sit so heavily in my stomach.

At least, I thought, I now understood enough about radioactivity to make some sense out of whatever a UFO hoax was likely to dish up.

I came back to a pink slip on my desk informing me that Karen had called and would I please call back. So I did.

"I've figured out that big red light those kids saw," she announced gleefully. "I went down to Target to see what I could find for a Halloween costume for Joey—he wants to be a pirate now, I hope he doesn't change his mind again—and they had those big plastic balls on sale, you know the kind, maybe ten inches in diameter and sort of translucent?"

"Uh, I think so."

"I bought one, to try it out, so it doesn't matter if you can't remember right now. I figure that if you took a bright flashlight and put it into the ball—they're stiff, you know, so they wouldn't collapse if you cut a hole in the side—you'd get exactly the effect of a big red light."

"Did you try it?"

"Well . . . almost. Our flashlight isn't all that strong, and I didn't want to cut a hole in the ball because I thought Joey would want to play with it, but yes, it seems to work."

"Wouldn't a balloon work just as well?" I asked, thinking of ease of disposal.

"Uh-uh. I tried that, too. The beam just goes right through; it doesn't give the right effect at all. The balls are much, um, thicker."

116

I thought I could picture what she meant. "Then you'd wave this thing around, and in the dark all people would see would be the light?"

"Maybe you'd have to be careful not to let the thing shine on you," she said. "I'm not sure about that."

"Well, it sounds possible, anyway."

"So that's almost all of it except the radioactivity," Karen said, sounding satisfied. "Prunella called this morning and I told her we were making progress."

"Did you say we thought it was a hoax?"

"Yes. Poor Prue. She was very disappointed." Of course she was; you don't found organizations like CATCH expecting to discredit every sighting that comes along. I made a sympathetic noise. "And I called Kurt Dixon about Rogers's car. I figured since he's a lawyer, he'd know what to do. He says he'll take care of it."

"Great!" At Kurt's ninety bucks an hour, I wondered what it would cost but didn't ask—whatever it turned out to be, it would be worth it to have the thing off my hands. I said good-bye and got back to work.

Just before five, I pulled into our newly empty garage and let myself in through the kitchen door. Saliva sprang into my mouth. "Hey, that smells good," I said.

"Hello yourself." Karen leaned against the faucet handles, and the torrent in the sink subsided. "Did you see? Somebody came and towed the car away."

"Fast work." From the family room came the familiar nasal bewilderment of Big Bird; I poked my head through the door to say hello to Joey as I shoved a hanger into my coat. When I turned from the closet, Karen had picked up a big, stiff envelope from the counter and was holding it out to me.

"This came this afternoon," she said.

The return address was Carleton College, with Ed Gustafson's friend's name scribbled above it. I tore the envelope down the front in my haste to see what the letter said.

A few fat Xeroxed pages were stapled together, and when I read the letter that went with them I was glad I'd taken my colleague to lunch that noon. "The only radioactivity in that sample that shouldn't have been there is from iron," I told Karen. "That's weird."

Karen flipped on the oven light and stooped to peer through the glass in the door. "How come?"

"How come it's weird? Because if something had made the iron in the dirt radioactive, you'd expect something else to be radioactive too."

"How could he tell it was only iron?"

"That's a long story," I said, sounding knowledgeable; I'd heard it that noon. "You know how each element has an atomic weight?"

"Sort of."

"Well, it does, and it depends on how many protons and neutrons are in the nucleus. But the way they sort elements out is by how many protons they have, and different atoms of the same element can have different numbers of neutrons. So you could have a whole bunch of things called iron, only their atomic weights are different."

"Some kinds of iron have more neutrons than others?"

"Right. I'm not sure how many isotopes of iron there are. That's what they call the different kinds, isotopes. The iron in this guy's report is iron-59."

"I guess I see," Karen said doubtfully. She rummaged in the refrigerator and came out with some thin plastic bags of vegetables. "How can they tell the radioactivity comes from iron, though? Why not uranium?"

"That's what I'm trying to explain." I crossed the room and got a knife and a cutting board to help her with the salad. "See, sometimes an atom has a combination of protons and neutrons that make it unstable. It gives off radiation until it converts to something else that is stable."

"Then it's not radioactive anymore?"

"Right. And while it's busy getting itself stable, it produces its own energy spectrum. That is, its individual, characteristic amount of energy." I thought that over and decided it would do. "Sort of."

118

"Like my jazzercise class. Some people really move and some sort of loaf along."

"Uh . . . I guess. Anyway, you can run a sample of a radioactive element through a scintillation counter, screen it for various energy levels, and come up with a pattern that matches the isotope you're looking at."

"Say again, in English?"

"Okay." I thought for a minute, trying to patch together my rusted-out college physics with what I'd learned at lunch. "Radioactivity is energy, like light is energy. In fact, think of it as light, that might make it easier."

Karen pursed her mouth and stared at the junction of the wall and the ceiling for several seconds. "Okay. I've got this light bulb."

"Well . . . Einstein might not recognize it."

"He's dead, anyway, so why would he care?"

"Point." I accepted the tomato she handed me, shook off the few remaining drops of water, and dug the stem scar out with the point of my knife. "Okay. You know that white light is made up of all colors, right?"

"I guess. Oh, yeah, prisms and rainbows and that kind of thing."

"Right. Well, say you're looking for something that absorbs a special color. You can put a sample of what you're wondering about into a machine called a spectrophotometer and shine a light through it and diddle around until you find out what color of light is absorbed by the sample. Then you know if it's the right stuff or not."

"I guess." Karen sounded unconvinced. "My education ran more to Milton than to Newton, remember."

"Like, if you've got a red solution in a tube, you shine a certain green light through it and if it's blood, it blocks the green light."

Karen sucked her lips in, frowning. "Okay," she said, the frown clearing. "I think I've got it. Each substance has its own special pattern of what color light it absorbs, and if what you run through your spectro-whatever-it-is matches that pattern, that's what you've got."

"Right. With radioactivity, it's a little different. The substance, the isotope, isn't absorbing energy; it's putting it out. You can put it into a thing called a scintillation counter and measure the energy put out over very small ranges, like each color of light is a small band of the whole rainbow. Once you find out where most of the energy is, you match it up with what you know about atoms and figure out what you've got."

"Oh," Karen said. "It's a *colored* light bulb! You should have said so before."

"Well . . . uh . . . yeah, sort of."

"What if you've got more than one kind?"

"That's the beauty of it. You can go down the whole range of energy levels and count each little band separately, one peak here, one here, one here"—I demonstrated by poking tomato, green pepper, and cucumber with the point of my knife—"and find out how much of each element you've got in your sample. And you not only know *if* it's there, you know what percentage of the whole sample it is, because you can compare it to what you get with a sample you know all about."

"Like counting up the lights on a Christmas tree and figuring out what percentage of them are green."

I blinked. "Sort of."

"And this sample had only one, what did you say, peak. For iron." I wanted to say that it showed the *pattern* for iron, but what with exercise classes, lightbulbs, blood, salad, and Christmas trees, I figured things were complicated enough already. "What's weird about that?"

"First of all, iron's pretty stable. You don't find radioactive iron in nature, like you do uranium. That means the iron we found had to sit in a nuclear reactor somewhere."

"The saucer."

"That's what we were supposed to think. But first, if the saucer had functioned as a reactor, if it exposed the ground to a neutron flux—"

"A what?"

Endless explanation stretched before me, obscuring my view of the Dixon's house next-door. The oven was making crackling and sizzling noises, the cucumber scent was strong in my nostrils.

"Forget it. Whatever it did, you'd expect lots of other elements to be radioactive too. Silicon, oxygen, carbon, bunch of stuff. But that didn't happen. So it has to be that the radioactive iron got onto the ground from some other place where it had been made radioactive." I stopped to picture that and laughed. "Can you see a flying saucer shedding radioactive rust?"

"I wonder what Ziebart would think."

"I see it slowly disappearing, like the Cheshire cat. But you do know what rust is, don't you?"

"That I do know." Karen folded a third napkin and put it beside Joey's plate. "Iron oxide."

"So why wasn't the oxygen radioactive too?"

Karen put the salad bowl on the table. In the family room, "Sesame Street" came to an end, brought to us by letters and numbers I couldn't quite hear.

"How deep was the ground radioactive?" Karen asked.

I picked up the Xeroxed sheets and looked to see which samples had shown the most radioactivity. "Not more than the top centimeter," I said. "That was the thinnest layer I could take."

The hot dish that had been simmering in the oven was transported to the table, an enticing aroma of garlic and thyme floating in its wake. "Oh boy, am I hungry," I said. "Joey?"

"Aw, can't I watch this?"

"No," called Karen. "Supper's ready. Go wash your hands and come to the table."

We had been eating for about five minutes when Karen said, "I guess what happened was that somebody scattered radioactive iron all over that circle. Is that what you thought?"

"Um," I said, around a mouthful of beef and macaroni.

"How?" She stared out the back window at the bird feeder for a moment, forgetting to eat. "With a spray gun? One of those bottles like Windex comes in?"

"You'd have to make a solution," I said.

"Where would you get the stuff to start with?"

"Out of the Yellow Pages, for all I know."

"I doubt it." Karen went back to her helping of casserole. After one mouthful, she asked, "Don't doctors use radioisotopes?

Like for thyroid disease? I think I remember reading about that in a magazine."

"That's iodine, not iron."

"Still. Somebody must use it. Iron, I mean."

"For what? Iron-poor blood?"

Joey shoved the last scrap of lettuce leaf into his mouth with his fingers and said, "Now can I go watch the rest of 'Three-Two-One-Contact'?"

"Sit up and finish chewing and ask to be excused," Karen said like a robot. To me: "Joe, that's what they did to the rabbit! They mixed the iron with its blood!"

"Karen, you don't just go mixing things with blood, even I know that. It clots. Besides, wouldn't the rabbit have to be alive?"

"I don't know." Karen nodded to Joey, who wriggled off his chair and dashed into the next room. "If somebody caught it in a Hav-A-Heart trap, though, I bet they could do anything to it that they could do to a lab animal, and that must include injecting things into its blood."

"When you put it that way . . . " I started to help myself to more hot dish, but the thought of the rabbit got in the way. "Maybe I'll call Powell and see what he thinks."

"No," Karen said suddenly. "Don't tell anybody. Nobody connected with this, not even him. Leave it to me—I'll find out."

"How?"

She smiled her mysterious smile. "I have ways," she said. "I'm a budding writer, remember? Everybody likes to help a budding writer, as long as they don't think you're going to write about *them*."

"What for?"

Karen grinned. "Their name in the front of the book."

XII

WHATEVER KAREN HAD in mind, I was distracted from it fairly quickly. The scratchy voice on the telephone later that evening belonged to Ed Gustafson, and he wasn't precisely happy.

"What's that guy Powell up to?" he demanded. "What's it got to do with you and that UFO?"

"I don't know," I said. "To both."

"You haven't talked to him, then."

"Not about what he's doing," I said cautiously. "Why, what's up?"

"Remember the *Clarion?* We bought a couple copies to put under that rabbit." Yes, a little weekly newspaper. "I dropped by with a write-up on that thing last weekend, and the editor—we go back a long ways—told me Powell was down here this morning wanting to see everything he had in his files on me, George Stemmermann, and Herm Miller. Not too charming about it either, he says. So?"

"I don't know, Ed. But I'll tell you, if you don't already know, they found a .22 rifle in Powell's van and confiscated it for tests."

"O-ho," Gustafson chuckled. "And what did he have that along for?"

"Pheasant hunting," I said. "He says."

A strangled noise came over the line. After a moment I realized that Gustafson was laughing. "You don't hunt pheasants with a .22!" he exploded finally. "I'm s'prised I didn't hear them laughing clear out to my farm!"

"I don't know what he told the sheriff, just what he told me." I repeated Powell's explanation of the rifle.

"Just about crazy enough to be true," Gustafson remarked, more soberly. "I don't know, though. . . . Something about it doesn't jibe. Can't put my finger on it. I wish I hadn't sent him copies of my witness interviews, though."

"What was he asking about at the *Clarion?*"

"I dunno. I guess he's got some idea I might have taken a pot shot at Rogers because he spoiled my UFO story just before elections. It wasn't my UFO story, but even if it was, what in hell does he think I am? Kill a guy because he spoiled a joke? I may be nuts, but I'm a good sport."

After a suitable pause, I said, "Sorry about this, Ed. Not my idea, believe me."

"For a semidecent member of the human race, you sure hook up with some weirdos, J.J.," Ed commented. "Give my regards to the wife, hey? And the little tyke."

"Sure thing. Keep me posted."

After that conversation, I suppose I shouldn't have been surprised when Powell showed up at my door a few minutes later, even though Rogers's murder had rated only three inches of space under a two-column headline at the back of the second section of his paper. "I've been down to Fox Prairie," he announced, tossing his coat over the back of a chair in the family room as if he lived there.

"I know."

He didn't appear to notice. "Talked to the sheriff. Damn it, they haven't got their ballistics report back yet—I mean, how long can it take to compare two shells?"

"Is that what they're comparing? Shells?"

Karen, in her corner of the couch, put her pen into the middle of her notebook and closed the cover over it. "Beer? Coffee?"

"Beer, thanks," Powell said. "Yeah, they found some shells along the side of the road there where that shooting took place. I guess the slug that was in him got too banged up to be much use as evidence."

"Couldn't you have done that by telephone?" Karen asked from the kitchen. She came back with three cans of beer and a plastic bag of potato chips that proved impenetrable until she went back for a knife.

"Had some other things I wanted to do, too," Powell said. He plunged his hand into the opened bag of chips.

"Excuse the elegant service," Karen said.

"What? Oh, this is fine. Just like home," he assured her, around the mouthful of chips. "Talked to the editor of a little weekly they've got down there, the *Clarion*. Had him pull all their info on Gustafson, Stemmermann, and Miller. What a wad!"

Considering that all three men had lived in or near Fox Prairie all their lives, and one was the high-school football coach as well as the principal, I wasn't surprised.

"Everything back to when they went marching off to World War II." Powell shook his head. "Other than that, stuff you've probably heard about Stemmermann. For a leading citizen, he sure has a knack for getting himself in trouble. Besides the current flap over his sexual habits, if any, he's had a bunch of drunk-driving arrests, and a few years back he got himself sued for draining a neighbor's pond by mistake. Nothing really criminal, at least that anybody ever proved. But he wouldn't like any more trouble, not at his age—that, I'd bet you anything."

"Everybody gets a run of bad luck now and then," Karen observed. She cocked her head as if she'd heard Joey stir in the bedroom down the hall, but she didn't get up.

"Miller, he's just a farmer. Did you know his father was trampled to death by his dairy herd back in the fifties?"

"I heard something about it."

"Now, that's really funny. In the barn, of all places. You don't hear of that happening often. Cows might get a little rambunctious when they're in heat, but a farmer with Miller's father's experience knows enough . . . "

Powell should know you don't shoot pheasants with a rifle! He knows too much else about rural living not to know that! I glanced at Karen. She was running one finger around and around the top of her beer can and sucking on her lower lip.

"What about Ed Gustafson?" she asked suddenly.

"Ah. Did you know our friend Gustafson has an election coming up?"

"An election! What on earth for?"

"Town council. They do things a little differently down there, I guess. Not like Minneapolis—no big election headquarters, no media blitz. I guess doorknocking could get a little wearisome too, if you had to go from farm to farm with your fistful of leaflets. I did see a couple of posters, Gustafson for Councilman, only I didn't make the connection. Area's full of Gustafsons."

"How about that," I said, for lack of anything better to say.

"He didn't mention it to you?"

I shook my head. "No reason he should, of course. I'm not voting in his district."

"Doesn't strike you that being connected with that sighting would be a lot of free publicity?"

Gustafson wrote the thing up. Handed it in to the newspaper. "No."

"And that he'd look like a damn fool sending for the high-powered bigshots from the city once the thing turned out to be a hoax? Besides it dropping out of the news too fast?"

"I can't see Ed doing that," Karen said.

Powell laughed. "Nobody's what they look like, don't you know that?" He slapped his knees. "So. That's what I've been doing today. What about you?"

"Not a lot," I began.

"I figured out how the guy made the red light," Karen said quickly. "Let me show you."

She went out to the kitchen again and came back with the flashlight we keep stuck to the side of the refrigerator by its magnet and reached into Joey's toy box for a large red plastic ball. "Watch this," she said, heading for the wall switch that controls the lamp beside the couch. In an instant we were in darkness. Then a light came on, a dimmish red ball of light. "How's that?" Karen asked.

"Pretty good."

The light bounced across the room, the effect only slightly marred by Karen's fingers under it, and moved behind the tendrils of the spider plant hanging near the window. A little shiver passed up my spine. The red ball bounced slowly back to the wall switch, and the lamp came on. "You'd need a stronger flashlight, of course," Karen said. "But you could get that at any hardware store. And if it were me, I'd cut a circle into the ball and stick the end of the flashlight in."

"Not bad," Powell said. "Simple, cheap—anybody could do it. I like that. Well, I've got some work to catch up on if I'm going to keep my job, so I'll be going. Thanks for the beer."

"Any time," I said, hospitably inane. Powell collected his coat from the back of the chair and let himself out. I put up the chain behind him and turned to Karen. "We didn't tell him about the letter about the radioactive dirt," I said.

"That's right. I said not to," she reminded me. "There's something not quite right about that man, and I plan to play my cards close to my chest."

"Can I peek?" I asked, stepping close.

"That's cheating," Karen said, but she didn't step away.

The next morning at work was one of those inexplicably slow ones that comes along once in a while. No one came to me with a crisis; no one wanted my rear end to warm a chair at a meeting, much less the attendance of my mind; nothing awaited my approval or rejection. The temptation was too much. I got out a pad of quadrille paper and started to make a list of the effects I would have to explain in order to have the Fox Prairie UFO fully reported.

Last on the list was the iron-59. Who would ordinarily use it, and for what? *Cameron Rogers would probably have known right away,* I thought.

Maybe his technicians would too. The university isn't that far from my office: the decision was made before I was even aware that I had framed the question. I told my secretary I might be back from lunch a little late and went down to the lot for my car.

I took only three wrong turns finding my way through a maze of hallways to Rogers's lab. Only when I had it in sight did it occur to me to wonder whether anyone would be there, now that the boss was gone for good. But I was in luck; the door was standing open and a young black woman with a long white apron looped over an ample bust and snugged around her jeans sat on a tall stool in the far corner of the room, working a black rubber bulb on a pipette to measure some kind of fluid into a rack of test tubes. She turned when I rapped on the doorjamb.

"Can I help you?"

"I'm looking for John Anderson."

"Bucky!" she bellowed, without getting off the stool. "Somebody to see you."

She went back to dribbling stuff into test tubes and I waited. No one came. The lab was clean and bright, with black countertops and gas cocks and sinks that seemed familiar from my college chemistry days, but more cluttered than any of the college labs had ever been. The green terrazzo floor looked a bit worn, yellowed around the bench bases and the junctures with the walls. After a couple of minutes the girl glanced at me again and yelled, "Bucky!"

A man came through a doorway on the opposite wall of the lab: John Anderson. Had to be, though he didn't match the picture I'd formed; far from the chinless wimp Rogers's comments had conjured up, this was a lithe Nordic about my own height, with a strong, angular jaw, brilliant blue eyes and a shock of hair the color of a straw broom. No way a loser. "Guy wants to see you," the girl said.

"Thank you, Angie." He was a little dry about it; emotional waves I didn't understand seemed to be washing at the walls of the stolid room. "Yes?"

"My name's Jamison," I said. "I'm the one who was working with Dr. Rogers on that UFO sighting when he, uh—"

"Bought it," Anderson finished for me, with no sign of emotion, either satisfaction or sorrow. "What can I do for you, Mr. Jamison?"

"I had some questions I thought Dr. Rogers could probably answer, but since he's . . . "

"No longer available," Anderson put into the blank I'd created with my hesitation.

"I figured maybe you could answer them just as well."

The girl in the corner snorted. Anderson smiled. "I'm certainly willing to try," he said affably. "Do you mind just pulling up a stool? I don't have an office."

128

I realized that the other room I could see through the door by which he'd entered must be part of the same laboratory complex. Sunday evening, Rogers had had all his equipment piled by the door I'd just come in and I hadn't seen the whole lab.

"We've discovered that the ground where that UFO supposedly landed is radioactive," I said. Anderson's eyebrows jerked. "But the radioactivity comes only from iron-59, so it appears that someone has spread some kind of radioactive iron-bearing compound over the surface."

"I don't know much about iron," Anderson murmured.

"Well." Suddenly, I was unsure what I wanted to ask. I'd hoped for a lead from Anderson, I realized, something to assist my ignorance. "I know radioactive isotopes are used in biological research and I'd hoped you'd know some of the uses of iron."

"'Fraid I don't," Anderson said. "We use some isotopes in this lab"—he pointed his chin at a red plastic case clipped to the lapel of his white lab coat. His name had been written on a piece of white cardboard showing through a window. Some way of measuring exposure, I guessed, maybe a piece of film?—"as what we call tracers. You hook them into the molecule you're interested in and then you can see where it goes in the organism, or in a reaction. I imagine iron could be used that way, too, though we're using cobalt, to trace vitamin B_{12}."

"But iron could be used in biological research."

"Oh, definitely." He grinned.

"So if someone had access to it, and wanted to—I don't know, maybe put it in an atomizer and spray it over an area, it could be done?"

Anderson wrinkled his forehead. "I'd guess so. I'd think he'd need rather a lot. That would make things pretty hot, though of course it could be transported in one of these." He stood up and reached under the lab bench near his feet and pulled out a lead cylinder. The top lifted off to reveal an empty cavity, with maybe three inches of lead around it.

"And whoever did it should take precautions, like using a face mask, for example." *Is he warning me?* I wondered. *Does he think I did it?* "Iron's important in a lot of biological compounds. Hemoglobin, for instance. It's stored in the liver, and once it's in your body, the only way it gets out is if you bleed it out."

"Oh, really." I congratulated myself on having worn the plastic sacks over my shoes. Maybe Miller had more of a problem than I'd thought.

"Of course, you realize that we're not talking about a lump of iron like an ingot. If it came from a biological laboratory, it would be in the form of a compound—soluble, probably—I'm not sure what. As I say, we don't use it here, and which compound it was would depend on what the researcher wanted it for."

"Yes, I can see that."

Anderson tried to push the lead cylinder under the bench with one foot, then gave up and edge-rolled it back into place with a two-hand shove, his back to me. "The chemistry of iron is pretty simple, as I recall," he said. "Once you had your compound, you could pretty well tailor it to any use you had for it. Like spraying out of an atomizer."

"Really."

"Any half-competent chemist could do it. Let's see. Both chlorides are soluble, I believe, and the sulphates." He raised his eyes to the glass-fronted cabinets above the bench where the girl was working. Brown jars of chemicals were lined up on the shelves, twenty feet of them.

"What about rust?"

"Oxides of iron? No. I'm assuming that whoever was planning this would try to disguise the source, since the presence of the compound he started with might be a giveaway. The whole thing's illegal, of course."

"Of course."

"Well, I hope I've been of some help to you, Mr. Jamison," Anderson said. "I'm sorry I was so distraught on the phone the other day—it was a shock, you know."

"I thought you recovered remarkably quickly," I said.

"A good technician has to function in a crisis." He smiled briefly and stuck out his right hand. I shook it. The last two

130

joints of the ring and little fingers were missing, I noticed, with the sharp drawing in of my groin that small deformities always cause. Anderson dusted his hand against the side of his lab coat. "Left them in 'Nam. The great American legacy of my generation," he said. "Lucky it wasn't my head, I figure."

"Sorry to see it," I said uncomfortably.

"Forget it." The abbreviated hand ducked into his coat pocket. "About your problem, if I can be of any further help, don't hesitate to ask. Here, I'll give you my home phone number." The hand popped out again to scribble on a pad of paper lying on the bench. He snapped off the top sheet and handed it to me.

"Thanks." I stuffed the paper into my shirt pocket. "Nice meeting you. Say . . ." *Keep your nose out of what doesn't concern you, J.J.,* my mother used to say, but I'm a slow learner. "What happens to the lab, now that Cameron Rogers is gone?"

"Oh, it stays, for a while, at least. He wasn't working alone, you know. One of his research associates will carry on."

"Is that you?"

"Me? No, I'm just a technician. I'll be getting my instructions from a doctor at the Mayo temporarily."

"Oh," I said. "Well, thanks again. And good luck." I smiled my nice smile and went back out the door of the late Cameron Rogers's laboratory.

"What you are, Bucky," I heard the girl say clearly, when I had taken maybe three steps into the hall, "is a turd."

XIII

POWELL HAILED ME from his van as I walked out of my plant at quitting time. "Get in for a minute," he said when I went over to the open driver's side window to look up at him. "Jeez, I never realized you guys would have a security guard on in the daytime. What do you make in there, bombs?"

"No." I crossed in front of the van and got in.

"What's with the guard, then?"

"We have our own secrets," I explained. "Ways we do things and products we're developing that we don't want our competitors to get hold of."

"Oh. I been sitting here half an hour waiting for you. Got any more info for me?"

I shook my head. "Sorry, I had to work today, you know."

"Yeah, I guess. What a drag." Powell stared at the bland brick plant as if he suspected it of being a front for a casino. "Well, lemme tell you what I've been up to. I got a background on Rogers."

"Oh?"

"Thought I'd spot some reason for getting rid of him. For a bastard, he's sure led a blameless life on the books."

"Good for him."

"Served in the army, picked up a bunch of medals, got a B.S. and his doctorate here at the U, went straight into the lab he was still working in as some kind of assistant. About ten years ago the guy in charge moved on and Rogers got his own grant as principal researcher. He's been in charge ever since."

"Oh."

"Never been married, never been sued for breach of promise, no DWI's. No outstanding parking tickets, even. Owns a condo downtown. The only thing to make him stand out from his nice, exclusive crowd is his interest in UFOs. Doesn't even get picketed

132

when one of the TV stations decides to investigate what nasty scientists are doing to defenseless rats. So I've got to believe that whoever killed him did it because of something connected with his interest in UFOs."

"He did have a temper."

"Don't I know it! But it doesn't seem to have landed him in any trouble. Not officially. His record's clean."

"Good for him," I repeated.

"So, what I'm wondering is, what can you tell me about Cameron Rogers and UFOs?" Powell, squinting against the sunlight that slipped into the van between the top of the windshield and the building in front of us, exuded sincerity. *He wants to know if I know something he doesn't want to get around,* I thought. *Something he thinks or knows Rogers knew.*

"I can't tell you, offhand," I said. "Why don't you come to the house this evening, oh, eight o'clock, and I'll get my computer to cough it up." I had my hand on the door handle, ready to jump.

"Okay," he said cheerfully.

"Good. I'll see you." I got out of the van and began my trudge to the edge of the parking lot, where I'd had to leave my car when I got back from lunch and found my usual spot taken, congratulating myself on getting off so easily. I should know by now that self-congratulation is an infallible sign that I've done something stupid; it took me until I had my hand on my own car door handle to realize that I'd just invited the man into my home, where not only I but my wife and small child were vulnerable. . . .

"No problem," Karen said. "I'll set it up with Celia Dixon. When Powell rings the doorbell, I'll call her and just keep talking until he leaves. If he dares try anything, I'll give her the code and she'll call the cops on Kurt's business line."

"Great! You think she'll mind?"

"Oh no. We've talked about it before, and I can see she's home." Looking suddenly worried, she added, "I hope she's not going out! I forgot it's Friday."

But the Dixons had planned a night at home. Powell came.

Karen and Celia had a long, chatty conversation, and Powell departed with about thirty pages of printout and effusive thanks.

"Now," Karen said, "let's just forget about this whole mess and pretend we're normal people."

Fine with me. And I had a good idea where to start. With the ball game on TV, of course. Where else?

I have a habit, when I'm given a name and a phone number, of looking them up in the telephone book to match them with an address. Karen tells me it's a sign of deep insecurity. Bull. I just feel wasteful if I leave blank lines in my address book, that's all.

So, when I found Anderson's slip of paper in my shirt pocket as I was dutifully removing the garment from the floor and putting it into the hamper the next morning, I decided to do my matching while Karen was off at the Country Store grocery shopping and not around to snicker.

The Minneapolis phone book has about eighteen pages of Andersons, but only four or five columns of Johns and plain J's. The St. Paul book has fewer than that. Matching my John Anderson with his address took less than five minutes. I copied both into my pocket address book and checked the running list of things to do Karen keeps posted on the refrigerator. *Fix back step.* Two stars. A good project for the morning, assuming that Jackson Powell left me alone. The telephone rang at the thought and I cursed.

Not Powell. "Mackenzie Forrester," I said. "Where the hell have you been keeping yourself?"

Nowhere unusual: on duty, he patrolled the streets of St. Louis Park, the suburb just west of Minneapolis where he's a cop; off duty, he stayed home with his wife and kids, but . . . "Our TV's on the fritz, J.J.," he said plaintively. "How's yours?"

"I might have known you wanted something," I said. "You want to come watch the game this afternoon, right?"

"Check."

"See you later." With Mack bringing his legendary thirst, I figured, I'd better get in a case of beer. As soon as Karen and Joey got home with the groceries.

*   *   *

Out Thirty-sixth Street there's a gas station that sells beer about as cheap as anywhere else in the city, and that was where I headed after helping Karen unload the station wagon. I could run up Fifth Avenue and stop at the lumberyard, too, I figured, and pick up a board to fix the back step. There'd never be nicer weather to do it. *The guy who set up that saucer landing lucked out on the weather too,* I thought. *He must have had everything ready to go whenever things looked good.*

Except the rabbit. How long could you keep that hanging around? That's what I should have asked Anderson. When I got home, I'd call him.

I was slamming the tailgate on my new board when I realized I was only four blocks from Anderson's house. *No time like the present. . . .*

The house was a nice one, small, in the Mediterranean style that usually looks so ridiculous here in the frozen North. This one was softened by plantings of evergreens instead of sitting like a Lego building on the lot, as that style often does. The black tile roof helped too; unusual, but more suited to our somber winters than the ordinary bright brick red. No toys in the yard, I noticed as I took the slate-paved path to the carved front door.

A woman with a scarf over lush blond hair answered my knock. "Yes?" she asked. Her eyelids blinked slowly over reddened eyes.

"Mrs. Anderson?"

"What do you want?" Suspicious. Maybe it wasn't a hangover; maybe she'd been smoking too much pot.

"I'm looking for your husband," I explained. "I—"

"He's not here."

"Oh. When—"

"He's not here, he hasn't been here for three months, and he's never going to be here. We're getting divorced."

Definitely pot. I could smell it on her bathrobe, now. "I'm sorry," I stammered.

"I'm not. You want his address, I guess. They always do." She stared past my left shoulder for a couple of minutes, blinking hard, then shrugged and turned away from the door. In a minute or two she reappeared with an address book. "Turning into a damn' secretary," she muttered as she flipped a page. She recited an address not far away, but in a neighborhood inhabited by students, old men, and what is politely called the "underemployed." Must have been a wrench for a man in his late thirties, with a steady job that had probably bought this small house, I mused as I wrote down the address. I wondered how often he gave out his old phone number out of habit.

"You won't get what he owes you, so you can forget that," the blond said. One of the carvings on the door smacked my elbow as she slammed it.

Momentum carried me back to the station wagon and onward the half mile to where Anderson now lived, but he wasn't there, any more than he'd been at his wife's house. He had a chunk of a shabby brick apartment building, three stories of boxes congealed into a single box. One was empty, the sign that said so already peeling its paint.

Half the yard was fenced, and a dog meandered around the corner of the house as I pushed back out the entrance door. It lifted a forepaw and stiffened when it saw me, sniffed suspiciously, and tried a few barks.

"Hello, boy," I said. The dog retired three steps, circled, and barked again.

"You like that dog?"

A stout old lady balanced between two shopping bags had come up the short walk. She regarded me warily; dog lovers obviously cut no ice with her.

"It's a nice-looking one," I said. It was, a medium-size dog almost the color of fresh beef liver, with silvery spots that blended into silvery paws and muzzle. It stopped barking and wagged its tail once or twice.

"Yah, pretty. Look at him. Pretty doggie, yah?" She glared at the beast to no apparent effect. "Daytimes, he's okay. Yah. Last weekend, then you should hear him. *Ya-oo-oo-ool,* all night long. I cou'n't sleep, downstairs cou'n't sleep. Left out ina dark, poor fella, not'in' to do but *ya-oo-oo-ool.*"

The dog, seemingly cowed by her vocal talents, sat down. "Whuf?" it said, looking at me. I shrugged.

"You looking at the apartment?" the woman asked anxiously, as if it had just occurred to her that she hadn't advertised the vacancy too well.

"No, I was looking for John Anderson."

"Oh, John, he's a nice boy," the woman said. "That's his dog. So he'll be back soon. After last Saturday, we all complained and he promised he wouldn't leave him out like that again. Poor fella." I wasn't sure whether she meant the dog or Anderson. "You know these young people, they're not like they were, they go out on a date and something comes up, they might stay at the lady's place over—" Something else occurred to her. "You one of the lawyers?"

"No." She nodded heavily and shuffled past me, the shopping bags ticking against the concrete walk at every step. Despite her promise, I gave up on Anderson—damn fool idea in the first place, and I did want to get that step fixed before game time.

As I unlocked my car door, I noticed something odd: down the block, a man in a small green car "reading" a newspaper so that it obscured his face. *Stakeout,* I thought, remembering some of Mack's stories. The temptation to sneak up and knock on the car window was strong, but I subdued it and went home.

Mack showed up around one o'clock and watched critically as I slopped some gray paint on the board I'd just put into the step. "You paint the underside before you put it on?" he asked.

I nodded at the warped and slightly rotten board I had removed, browned on the underside but totally devoid of finish. "Yes."

"Good boy." He stepped over the fresh paint and onto the porch. "Karen home?"

"Uh-huh."

"You won't mind if I walk in and get myself a beer, then." The back door was standing open; Mack swung the screen open as he spoke and let it slam behind him.

Putting away and cleaning up took a few minutes; the game

had already started by the time I joined Mack. He'd appropriated, as usual, my recliner, and this time my son as well—Joey, holding his fielder's glove, had squirmed into the seat beside him. I dropped onto the couch and popped the top on a beer of my own.

"Hear you've put your foot in it again," Mack said. "Can I count on you to count me out?"

"You mean Rogers?" The beer was a little flat, not cold enough yet, and the potato chips in an opened bag I'd scrounged out of a cupboard near the sink were soggy. I gave them to Joey after so little pleading that he frowned into the bag and picked out the smallest one to sample.

"Check. I won't get sucked into this one, will I?" Mack asked.

"Not as far as I know," I assured him. "I'm still sorting out the UFO somebody wanted us to think landed down there, but the sheriff's in charge of the other investigation and that's just fine with me."

"I should hope so." The first three batters had gone down in order. Mack allowed himself a soft, throaty cheer as the team he was rooting for jogged in from the field. The TV cut to a beer commercial, which is where all ball players seem to go sooner or later.

"He doesn't think there's any connection?" Mack asked, while some former pitcher made his new pitch.

"I guess not." I embarked upon a summary, in words too long for Joey to understand, of the sheriff's theory about hunters as distinguished from killers, but the game came back on and Mack didn't seem to notice when I stopped in midsentence.

"Sounds reasonable," he said while the lead-off batter trotted back to the dugout. "From what I read in the papers, that setup would have taken some pretty detailed local knowledge, and who could be sure Rogers would go for it? He might have called in one of the local boys, or maybe even settled for sending you. Hey, maybe it was meant for you!"

"That's what I like about you, Mack. You make a guy feel so secure. Must be the uniform."

"I'm not in uniform."

138

"Right."

I was saved from whatever Mack might have thought by a double to left field. The can in Mack's paw crinkled at the crack of the bat, and ten seconds later the guy on the screen was jumping up and down on second base, dusting his pants off. That put the cleanup batter on deck, Mack pointed out an instant before the play-by-play man did, equally unnecessarily.

"What does he have to clean up?" Joey wanted to know.

"Did I tell you?" Mack asked, when the game was over. "I'm thinking of going back to school."

"For what?"

"Law."

Karen, who had joined me on the couch around the middle of the seventh inning, folded her arms. "What about your job?" she asked.

"My job." Mack's face lengthened; for an instant he looked like the high-school kid I'd horsed around with on the school bus years before. He glanced at Karen and then out at the backyard, where Joey and a couple of other kids were giving the swings a workout. "You know about my job."

"I thought you liked it," Karen said.

"I do. I like the idea of it, maybe . . . but. . . . Jeez, Karen, do you know what I did this past week? I rode around in the dark in my car with my belly hanging out over my belt a little farther every mile. I arrested some old guy got too drunk to zip his fly and forgot to tidy himself up after he went to the john. I picked up an *eight*-year-old—same age as my Mary Ellen—for shoplifting a couple of tapes out at Target. I stopped four drunk drivers. One of them stuck his fist in his ear and thought he was calling his lawyer. When he couldn't hear the phone ring, he accused me of pulling out the phone line!"

Karen giggled.

"Yeah, it would read funny in *Reader's Digest,* maybe, but it was no joke at the time, I'll tell you. Night before last I went looking for a prowler that wasn't there. The same one, three times. I told somebody's neighbor to keep his dog in his own yard. I told somebody else's neighbor to turn his stereo down—

the complainant was too scared to go over and tell the guy to do it himself, and you know what? Turned out to be some geezer around ninety years old; all he said to me was, 'Hanh?' so I turned the music down myself, and then *he* put in a complaint. I wrote reports on all that junk. Christ, did I write reports!"

I sang, "A policeman's lot is not—"

"Shut up."

"There's boring stuff in any job, Mack," Karen said. "Joe complains about it all the time, and I get pretty sick of retyping things, myself."

"Yeah, but you don't have to worry about whether your typewriter's gonna pull a knife on you," Mack pointed out. He stopped and looked at the television, where the theme for the early-evening news had started. "Hell, you don't want to hear all this," he said. "Forget it. Mind if I stay long enough to catch the weather? Then I'll run along home."

"You want to watch tomorrow's game?" I asked.

"Can't." He smiled tightly. "There's constabulary duty to be done."

The news started with a report on a murder case that had been dragging through its investigation for the better part of the summer, stymied because the body of the victim hadn't been found, and under Minnesota law they have to have the body before they can bring charges. Now they'd found the body, in a hayloft on an abandoned farm.

"See?" Mack said. "Even the exciting cases get boring. By the time you get to court with something . . . "

A young black woman, identification withheld pending notification of relatives, had been beaten to death near her Dinkytown apartment. She'd bought a quart of beer and pretzels at a nearby convenience store just a few minutes before, and she'd also been stabbed with the smashed bottle. Nobody had spotted her assailant. "And stuff like that," Mack said. "Some kid walks home in the twilight and a goon jumps out of an alley and that's it. Takes it out of you, you know?"

The anchorman went on to report that a squad car had been within three blocks of the crime when it occurred but that no

140

one had called the police. "How do you think the guy in that car feels today?" Mack commented.

"Well, he can't blame himself for something that's not his fault," Karen said tartly.

"I'm not talking about blame. I'm talking about how helpless you get to feeling sometimes."

"Why study law, then?"

"It's the only thing I know anything about." Mack fell silent and we watched the rest of the news: three or four international stories, a picture story about a festival nearby. Fair and warm weather promised.

"Well," Mack said. "Thanks, J.J." He got up and gathered the empty beer cans into his big hands and carried them out to the kitchen. "Nice seeing you, Karen. You and J.J. ought to come over some night when I'm not on duty, check? We've been talking about having you over. Joey, too. He could play with Mickey and Dustin and sack out on their floor when he gets tired."

"Sounds good," I said. "Play some bridge?"

"Why not? Joy'll call you. Stay cool, you two." He pushed through the screen door and cursed.

Stepped on my new board, naturally. First-quality oil-base paint, still nice and tacky. "That's okay," Karen said through the screen. "A little grit will give it some traction when it rains."

Sure. She didn't have to repaint it.

XIV

"YOU KNOW SOMETHING? I haven't seen Jackson Powell all day," I remarked later that evening.

"Shhh," Karen replied. "You don't want to attract him, do you?"

"Not on your life." I reached into the refrigerator for a can of beer, and the phone rang.

"See what you did?"

"Okay, okay. I'll get it." I tucked the can I'd been about to pop under my arm and picked up the telephone.

"Hello, is Karen Jamison there, please?" asked a voice I thought I should recognize. Brisk, male, no-nonsense. Not Jackson Powell. I held the receiver out to Karen, said, "For you," and went back to my favorite chair and picked up the book I'd been reading.

"Hi, Doctor," Karen said.

And that, for the moment, was all. I waited a young eternity while she made small sounds that signaled that she was still on the line. Her back was toward me, but she stood relaxed, a shoulder against the door frame, so I popped the top of the beer can and tried to pay attention to the book in my lap. The beer was too cold, and the book too uninteresting to distract me from the sudden cold pain in my front teeth. I gave up on both and listened to Karen's end of the conversation.

"What happens to it then?" she asked, after a few minutes. The answer was a long one.

"Yes, I think I understand," she said. "And it would be easy to do? . . . Sure, you'd need the right equipment. Where? . . . Oh. What about an anesthetic? . . . Oh, *really?*" She pressed her free hand just under her breasts and half-turned toward me. She sounded flabbergasted. "They just hold still? . . . I don't think this one would have, it was wild. . . . Uh-huh. Okay, I'll send you a letter, would that be okay? . . . Fine. Thanks so much, I really appreciate this."

She hung up and returned to her corner of the couch, where she folded her legs under her and grasped one ankle and stared at me.

"Why the doctor?" I prompted.

"I asked him about that rabbit we saw. The one in Fox Prairie, not the one that ate my asters."

"Wouldn't a vet be more appropriate?"

"Probably. But I don't know any vets." She sucked in her lower lip. "Maybe not. Let me tell you what he said, will you?" I nodded. "I asked him about the radioactive iron, how it could get into the rabbit. He says we should check whether the rabbit is radioactive all through, or if somebody planted something in one place."

"We haven't got it."

"I know. *Assuming* that it's radioactive all through—he said to take several samples of muscle tissue and check each one—there's a way you can hook the radioactive iron onto red blood cells. He explained it all, but I'm afraid I didn't quite get it, and he's been so nice about looking this up I hated to take any more of his time. Something to do with antigens and antibodies. You make the antibodies radioactive somehow. Anyway, what you do is get some blood from the rabbit and treat it so the antibody with the iron is stuck on the red cells and then you inject it back in. It only takes a few seconds to circulate through the whole body, and then the whole animal is radioactive. Except for its fur and nails, he says."

"How do you get that much blood from a live rabbit?"

"Straight out of its heart, he says." She folded her hands in a V above her breasts.

"Sounds gruesome." I thought of a coronary-bypass operation I'd seen on TV once, a confusion of reds and pinks and yellows, bathed in blood. No wonder the beast had been so cut up!

Wrong. "You can do it from outside, he says, with a big hypodermic needle," Karen explained. "It doesn't even hurt very much, he says, and some rabbits will just lie still for it after

143

they've had some experience, though usually a second person holds them down, poor beasts."

"Does that mean we have two people to look for?" I wondered aloud.

"No. He says that if someone's working alone, there are ways to restrain the animals so they don't have to worry about them wriggling around and messing themselves up."

"This . . ."

"Cardiac puncture," Karen supplied.

"It doesn't kill them?"

"He says no. He says you can do it over and over and the rabbit's still okay." She got up and retrieved the *TV Guide* from the top of the television and looked at it with a worried frown. "Oh, I almost forgot. I asked him what happens to the blood after you do all this and inject it back into the rabbit. He says the cells are damaged by the treatment, so the liver and spleen capture them and destroy them. Pretty fast, too. So I guess they'd be more radioactive than the rest of the body?"

I thought about that for a minute or two. "So that if somebody like Cam Rogers noticed it, he'd figure out right away what had been done," I concluded. "So they had to be taken out, and then all that other stuff had to go too, to hide the fact that it was the liver and spleen that mattered." I shuddered.

"It's almost like a dare," Karen remarked.

"Maybe." I wasn't convinced. I've seen plenty of "little jokes" set up by people desperate for attention, or who wanted to pull somebody's leg and have a good laugh, and none of them deliberately planted clues.

Though, come to think of it, if the person you wanted to trick was an experienced researcher, a missed clue or two—especially if it was something he'd be sure to have come across before—would make the laugh all that much better . . . and if Karen was right, didn't that prove the hoax and the murder were separate things? Because you couldn't enjoy your laugh on the guy if he was dead. Rogers might have pushed somebody already teetering that one more step over the brink of murder, and somewhere somebody, maybe more than one somebody, who had gone to a good bit of trouble to manufacture a UFO

144

for Rogers's benefit was castigating himself for an unintended death, too scared to come forward. As I might have been myself. But who?

"Did he say what they use the stuff for?"

"Experiments. Tracing molecules through a system. Iron-59 has even been used to track red blood cells by this exact method, he said, as long as twenty-five years ago."

I nodded. That meant someone who knew about that, didn't it? John Anderson? No. How would he know about Herm Miller's field? Someone who'd run across Rogers in his other UFO investigations? More likely. I'd better ask my computer for another printout on Cameron Rogers and UFOs like the one I'd given Jackson Powell.

Stemmermann. Would someone who set up an eavesdropping system be likely to enjoy a good laugh on a man of Rogers's reputation? Hmmm....

"You know what's next," Karen said. "We have to find out who's missing some of this radioactive iron."

"Almost has to be from the Twin Cities, don't you think?"

"Or from Northfield, if someone at Carleton is using it and hasn't noticed some missing . . . "

Or is in on the joke and has a friend in Fox Prairie.

"Or from Rochester! My God, the Mayo Clinic! Didn't you say Anderson was getting orders from somebody there?"

"Someone who had been working with Rogers, right," I said, getting excited. "That's a definite possibility!"

"Wherever it came from, it came recently," Karen said. "The doctor told me it only has a half-life of a month and a half, and if it was as weak as you say, it might have been undetectable in another couple of weeks."

"How could we find out where it came from?" I stared at the telephone, but it didn't shake any ideas loose.

"Wouldn't they report it to the police if it was stolen?" Karen asked. "Maybe Mack could help."

"Good idea. I'll give him a call right now." The book I'd been reading slid off my lap onto the floor as I stood, I'd forgotten it so completely. Karen rescued it with a little cry and tried to smooth out the bent pages while I went to the phone to call Mack.

He hadn't heard of any missing isotopes. He extracted a long explanation of my interest and promised to look into it the next day, as long as I guaranteed that he wasn't going to get snarled in my investigation. "Absolutely not, if you don't want to be," I said. "I'm only trying to pick your brains. Say, that reminds me. You remember one time telling me about something called postmortem hypostasis? Would there be any way to fake a pressure mark with that? Of a stick, say?"

"Your rabbit? Sure, all you need is another stick."

We chatted on for a minute or two, but I hung up deep in thought. All you'd need is another stick. Somebody had scouted that site very, very carefully indeed. I shook off the mental image of the rabbit and turned on the TV for the late news.

Much the same as at six. The body in the hayloft had been identified as the missing woman's. The woman in the alley, one Tabitha A. Brent, proved to have been bludgeoned with an aluminum baseball bat found thrust down a storm sewer in the next block; no wars had been settled, but no new ones had started. Two guys with a Cessna full of cocaine had been arrested in a field near Owatonna. The weather forecast remained fair and warm, with threats of rain for Monday. Myself, I was ready for bed and hoping I wouldn't dream too clearly.

"Joe," Karen said tentatively. "Fox Prairie isn't all that far from Owatonna, is it?"

"Few miles." My ears cracked with a yawn I didn't bother to cover. "Why?"

"What was that Cam said, about stuff hiding in little nooks?"

"When?"

"When we were looking at that pottery in that little shop window. On our way back to the school after lunch?"

Yes. "I think that's all he said, that you'd be shocked at the stuff hiding in some of these little nooks."

"Joe . . . why *shocked?*" She caught her lower lip under her front teeth. "Could he have overheard something about that cocaine deal coming up?"

146

"Where would he overhear it that we wouldn't?" I asked. "We were with him all the time."

Karen let her head fall back against the back of the couch, eyes closed. "No," she said. "It only seemed that way. Before dinner that first evening, breakfast the next morning . . . "

I could see his smirk, the tanned lower lid of his left eye rising as the right eyebrow flicked upward and he said . . . what? Something about hicks.

"He said something about Fox Prairie not being the innocent outback it pretended to be . . . something he'd overheard at breakfast. And Joe, he said it had been a profitable morning." Karen ran both hands into her hair and clutched at the sheafs of curls that stood up. "After you were done with the interviews. It came over the intercom. Stemmermann was there, and the school clerk. Good God, Joe, for all I know the whole school heard it!"

"I doubt that."

"That fussy, dumpy little man?" Karen got up and turned off the oblivious sportscaster. "Cocaine?"

"You mean Stemmermann? Karen, we haven't proved anything. We don't even know if Rogers knew anything about the cocaine."

She wasn't listening. "He's got a nose, such as it is, and I guess he could use it for anything anybody else could. Omigod, those kids on that football team!"

"Karen, have you ever heard of a house of cards?"

She sighed, short and sharp, and glanced at me. "Right. I'm really building on sand this time. All the same . . . " She reached under the skirt of the recliner and retrieved a small black Lego block that had been disguised in its shadow. "I think you should call the sheriff and tell him about it. It sounds like Rogers, doesn't it? To try to muscle in on something like that?"

"Does it? The man wasn't an idiot," I pointed out. "People smuggling drugs don't just welcome strangers into the deal with open arms."

"Joe, you remember the way he was after that . . . that incident with Jackson Powell. What's the word the English use? Cocky. As if nothing he did would ever get him in trouble.

Then, there was the person he recognized in the Home Kitchen. Someone from the Twin Cities, maybe? A buyer?" She stared at me. "I still think you should call the sheriff."

I hesitated a moment. Karen has been right so many times, it's hard to dismiss her theories, slenderly built as they sometimes are. "In the morning," I said finally. "For now, come to bed."

"All right."

Such enthusiasm!

I postponed the call until I'd had a Sunday breakfast of oatmeal muffins, cranberry juice, and coffee. The guy answering calls took my message and assured me that somebody would look into it. He sounded even less interested than I was. But duty had been done, so I went out to the garage and grabbed a rake to work on the leaves our elm trees had dumped on the lawn.

The sun was warm on my back, the crisp scent of the leaves acrid in my nostrils, mingled near the flower border with the spicier odor of Karen's prized chrysanthemums. It was a day for good muscle work; I didn't mind raking the same leaves into a pile four or five times for Joey and his best friend Gary to jump into and roll in, and when the bigger kids' football bounced into the yard I fielded it and threw it back to the game in the street, pleased with the feel of arm, shoulder, and belly working together. The pleasure stayed with me up until the blue van with the sunburst rear window crunched through the dry leaves in the gutter across the street and came to a stop.

"Hey, J.J.!" Jackson Powell called. "Got a minute?"

The football game had stopped, the gangly boys standing around staring at me and Powell. "Sure," I said.

He slammed the van door with a tinny clunk, lifted a hand to excuse himself through the middle of the resuming game, the grin of a dissolute cherub back on his face. "Hey, did you hear about that cocaine bust near Owatonna yesterday?"

"Yeah, it was on the news last night. Coffee?" I stood the rake beside the front door and led the way in. "Karen? Jack Powell's here," I called.

148

"Miss me yesterday?" he asked, still grinning.

"Not much."

Powell laughed. "I had to drive down to Faribault and interview some guy who carves stumps into fat ladies with a chain saw and sells them for a thousand bucks apiece. Like one of his neighbors says, 'I wouldn't pay that if she was real!' There's where the money is, J.J. Get yourself one of those jobs the beavers are so sold on, beg a few elm trunks from the city when they're cutting them down, and you could make yourself a nice little nest egg. Beats working for a living."

"Was he deaf?"

"The guy who does the carving? A little, now you mention it. Hi, Karen."

Karen was already fitting a filter into the top of the coffeepot. "I figured you couldn't talk without fuel," she said.

"Good woman!" He turned back to me. "Then yesterday afternoon, that was my afternoon with my kids. Took them and my sister's boy over to Como Park to feed some seals and watch the polar bears splash. So I'm still in the same spot I was last time I saw you. You made any progress?"

Behind his shoulder, Karen's warning frown. "Not so's you'd notice," I said. "I don't think there's much I can do."

"I'm still ready to help you," Powell said, "though I'm wondering if maybe that cocaine bust takes me off the hook." He sat down and curled one hand around the other fist, resting his forearms on the tabletop. "You don't know if Rogers might have overheard something about that shipment coming in, do you?"

You don't sell two kilos of cocaine in rural Minnesota. You sell it in the Twin Cities. And maybe you need somebody to come down and pick it up, somebody with a reasonable excuse for being there, like a reporter. "If he did, he didn't tell me about it," I said.

"Shit. Well, there goes that idea. Thanks." He took the mug Karen held out to him.

The shipment doesn't come through on Tuesday, when you first planned it, so the reporter covers his ass by looking at a possible UFO story. Which just conveniently happened to turn up? Sure.

"Milk?" Karen asked.

"Thanks." Powell reached out for the pitcher. The tear in the sleeve of his battered jacket had been neatly mended. *When somebody roughs the guy up a little, he doesn't dare make a fuss. . . .*

"Sugar?" Karen asked.

"No, thanks." Powell patted his well-padded belly.

The delivery gets rescheduled for Thursday and back the reporter goes. Something else goes wrong, so he raises a little hell in a newspaper office—after all, he's a reporter. . . .

"That your daughter, out on the swing?"

Karen glanced out the back window. "No, she's from down the block. Joey's around somewhere, I think watching the big kids play football."

Saturday, the stuff is finally coming. You cover that with the interview in Faribault, which is what, fifteen miles north of Owatonna on the interstate?

"Naturally, I had to miss that cocaine bust, while I was looking at the other busts," Powell said. "I must have been within twenty miles of the action. One of these days I'm going to find myself a stringer for a gardening magazine, bragging about my glory days on the big-city paper. First Rogers, now this." He shook his head. "Talk about a nose for news. Mine has chronic sinus trouble."

If the transfer comes off, fine. If it doesn't, you're a reporter with a hot tip working on a story. . . .

"You look thoughtful, J.J.," Powell said.

"Sorry." I forced a yawn, which turned into a real one. "A little sleepy, is all."

"If you're a baseball fan, you'd better wake up quick," Powell chided. "Game starts in fifteen minutes, and this could be it." He drank half of his coffee. "Say, have you got a copy of the interviews Ed Gustafson did before you and Rogers went down there?"

"Sure."

"Read it yet?"

150

"Skimmed them, anyway. I didn't see anything new. Why?"

"He sent me copies. You know what? Every single witness to that light went past the place in a compact car."

"Nobody walks down there," I said.

"No, no. You don't get it. Where were the pickups? Where were the vans, the full-size cars? It doesn't make sense, *unless*"— he smiled mirthlessly—"unless the guy doing it figured trucks and big cars might be more likely to stop to see what was up. And have guns in them."

"You might have a point there," I said.

"Sure I do. Shows that whoever did that knew a little bit about what goes on in October in backwoods Minnesota." Powell got up and stretched, excused himself by reminding us of the tropism that would draw half the American populace to the TV set on that glorious afternoon, and left.

"You get the feeling we were being pumped?" Karen asked.

"Could be."

"I'm just as glad we kept quiet. Something about that man . . . I don't know. I just don't trust him. Lunch?"

"Lunch."

She slipped something into the microwave and went to the door to call Joey in to wash his hands.

I knew right away that the caller was Lydia Eskew. It's not that she's hard of hearing. It's just that she doesn't quite trust the telephone company to get her voice over the wire with enough oomph to be heard. Karen held the receiver away from her ear and made a face at me, where I sat at the kitchen table finishing a second helping of warmed-over lasagna.

" . . . not so nice this time," I heard Mrs. Eskew say. "But you'll have to go there again. Sometime when there aren't any flying saucers to trouble you and people aren't shooting one another. It's really quite a lovely—what's that, Sarah?"

Karen grinned at me, a silent laugh, while mutterings came over the line from the house next-door. "Sarah thinks," came the renewed blast, "I'm making Fox Prairie sound like a nineteenth-century border town. Which, of course, it was. She

151

says people hardly ever shoot—what? Oh, *never* shoot each other down there. What's that, Sarah?"

Karen slid her right hand stiffly up her left cheek and rubbed at the little hollow just in front of her ear.

"Sarah says you should come over this afternoon for a cup of tea, and she'll tell you all about the town. I bet she could even tell you who set up that terrible joke."

"That sounds lovely," Karen replied, unconsciously adopting Mrs. Eskew's turn of phrase. "When would you like us to come?"

"Oh, any—what's that, Sarah?" Karen leaned against the counter with one arm folded across her middle, gazing at the ceiling with the half-repressed smile of a woman who sees the punchline coming.

"Around three?" Mrs. Eskew said, so loudly that even I jumped. I nodded.

"That's fine, Mrs. Eskew," Karen said. "We'll be there, as long as you don't mind if Joey runs in and out."

"Oh, heavens, no," Mrs. Eskew boomed, and Karen put the phone back on the hook and rubbed her ear. "I think she's getting worse," she said. "Old age, do you think?"

"Possible." I stood up and put my plate in the sink. "I ought to give myself a medal for agreeing to that, is what I think," I said. "I'm going to miss the end of the World Series."

"No, you won't." Karen put on her mysterious smile. "You'll see."

At three o'clock I discovered that my neighbor, a woman I'd known for years, was secretly one of those baseball fans whose fervor is aroused one week out of the year—something I suppose I'd have known sooner if I hadn't been watching the games myself all that time. The television was on, the volume low, and both of the old ladies leaned toward it from their perch on the edge of the sway-backed old couch as Karen and I peered through the screen of the open front door.

"Come on in, it's on the latch," Mrs. Eskew said. We pushed into her dim parlor just as an ad for razor blades was unleashed.

"Top of the fifth," Mrs. Eskew announced. "Are you following the World Series, J.J.?"

"Sort of," I lied.

"Then I'll leave the sound on," Mrs. Eskew decided briskly, seeing right through me. "You can keep track of the game while Sarah talks to Karen." She herself, it appeared, would assist me in keeping track of the game.

"Lydia," the other old lady said tentatively.

"Oh, yes, sorry, I forgot. You don't know one another, do you? This is Sarah Burnham, Reuben's sister," Mrs. Eskew said hurriedly, bustling out to her kitchen as she spoke. "Karen and J.J.," she finished as she disappeared.

"Pleased to meet you, Mr. and Mrs. . . . ?"

"Jamison," Karen supplied. "How do you do?"

"Why don't you sit here, Mr. Jamison?" Sarah Burnham indicated the cushion next to her with a graceful wave. "You can see best from there."

She was older than her sister-in-law, less compact and more fragile-looking; a tall, angular woman whose scanty flesh hung from her arms and whose face and arms were blotched with age. In her light wool dress she looked ready to put on her hat and gloves and step into a limousine, with a gracious nod of thanks to someone holding the door for her; her big-knuckled hands sported rings on three fingers, one of them a wedding band worn almost to the point of invisibility. The couch received me like a large, soft bucket.

"The lead-off batter is on base," said the TV.

"My, isn't that nice," said Sarah Burnham.

"What happened? What happened?" her sister-in-law demanded, setting down a tray loaded with tea things so abruptly it clattered.

"Just an infield single, Lydia; do try not to smash your pretty cups."

Was it there that the afternoon became surreal? If not, it had plenty of other opportunities. I sat back in the sagging couch cushions, knees awkwardly raised, trying to balance an embroidered napkin and a small porcelain plate wreathed in infinitesimal pink flowers, holding a matching saucer and a cup

153

whose handle wasn't large enough to fit even one finger through and which Mrs. Burnham kept supplied with progressively stronger tea, munching on madeleines while Mrs. Eskew and her late husband's sister instructed me—with surprising canniness—in the tactics of baseball. Karen, who had wisely chosen a straight chair, juggled tea and cookies and crockery without turning a hair, and, to her credit, managed not to smirk at me against what must have been vast temptation.

"Edward Gustafson used to play baseball," Sarah Burnham remarked. "Semiprofessionally, I believe. But when his father died, he came back to manage the farm."

"He's the one who called you about the flying saucer, isn't he?" Mrs. Eskew said brightly. I was quite certain she'd already filled her sister-in-law in on every detail I'd told her about, so it didn't matter that we all paused to watch the televised flight of a small white ball into the upper deck, at the last moment hooking foul.

"My, he was a wild one," Mrs. Burnham continued, when the crowd noise had died to a disappointed murmur. "But he settled down after a while. Nothing like getting up before five every morning to settle a man down, I do say. Cows have a wonderfully insistent influence." She smiled a little smugly. "They dislike being cussed at, too, I've heard."

Karen glanced at me, a little glance of disbelief. "Ed certainly seems well-settled now," she said.

"Oh, dear, yes. Quite stodgy in his middle age, I'm afraid. Lydia, dear, the pot's gone empty. Shall I start some more water?"

"I'll do it during the next ad," Mrs. Eskew said.

"Such a prankster Ed was." Mrs. Burnham's mouth twisted into a sly little smile and her faded brown eyes took on a sparkle. "One time he ran a set of red longjohns—you do know what they are, don't you?—a set of red longjohns up to the top of the high-school flagpole. Then he shinnied up and tied off the rope at the top, so they couldn't be lowered, and he greased the pole on the way down! My, such consternation! They had to get in a crane from a construction company working in Rochester to get the longjohns down. Meanwhile they flapped up there for three whole days! 'Course, Ed didn't admit he was any part of it until years and years later, but people were still talking about it when I first moved to Fox Prairie, over forty years ago."

Not more than a couple of years after it happened, I figured. On the screen, the pitcher caught a pop fly and lobbed it over his shoulder as he ran for the dugout. The game was over.

"Seven–two," Mrs. Eskew announced the score. "Do you want to watch them bathe each other in champagne?"

"No thanks," Karen said. Mrs. Eskew got up and turned the television off.

"Well," Sarah Burnham said, with an air of finality. "Until next year!" She raised her empty cup in a mock toast and set it down. "Now. Who else did you meet in Fox Prairie?"

Joey appeared at the screen door, the triangle of his forehead and nose darkened as he pressed his face against the screen. "Hey, Dad, the game's over," he said.

"I know."

"Can I go to Gary's house?"

"Be home at five-thirty," Karen said. "Okay?"

"George Stemmermann," I said to Sarah Burnham.

"The school principal," she replied, nodding. "Not a well-liked man, I'm afraid. Mr. Burnham's younger brother was at school with him. The sort of little boy who pulls the wings off flies, though I don't suppose he does it anymore. Still, people don't believe good of a person shaped like that. Pity, isn't it?"

"What I don't understand is how he got to be a football coach."

"Oh, I believe he played in high school. And he used to teach physical education, back when I was first in Fox Prairie—he was somewhat sleeker then, you see. Lydia, dear, the kettle's been whistling for ages."

"I'm going, I'm going."

"You've never heard anything, uh . . . "

"Detrimental?" Mrs. Burnham supplied smoothly. "Oh, no. Of course, you do know he never married."

Living with Karen, I'd almost forgotten how much nuance can be put into a simple phrase. Even I, slow as I am about these things, caught this one. Dumpy Coach Stemmermann, damned because he never married. Maybe none of the elegant Fox Prairie ladies had cared to join him in matrimony, I thought.

Mrs. Eskew carried the teapot back into the room, supporting it gingerly by its spout as well as its handle, and refilled all our cups.

"And Herman Miller," I said. "He's the one who owns the field the UFO is supposed to have landed on."

"Herm Miller! Oh my goodness." Sarah Burnham's mouth twisted again into that sly little smile. "And he and Ed such good friends." She stopped and sighed. "But poor Herm has had his share of woe; I suppose he's entitled to have a bit of fun."

"Not so much fun," Karen said, a trifle sharply. "The ground where the thing landed is radioactive, and he's afraid for his grandchildren."

"Radioactive!" Mrs. Burnham's delicate eyebrows arched prettily as she dipped her head in one slow nod. "That *was* naughty. But the children, they still visit every summer, do they?"

"The grandchildren? That's what we've heard."

"A pity. A pity." She reached for the last of the madeleines and nibbled it reflectively. "Not that they visit him—that's only natural. I mean that his daughter turned out so unstable. She left her first husband, you know."

"We'd heard," I said, maybe too dryly.

"And those two adorable children—well, Herm knows what it is to lose a parent; his mother died when he was quite young and then there was that terrible accident with his father." She sighed. "Farming is such a dangerous occupation! Most people have no idea."

We observed a moment of silence to contemplate the very real dangers of farming.

"So Herm keeps up with the children's father, of course. He often visits them when they're at the farm, even now that he's remarried. Herm says it just isn't right to keep a child from its father, even if it is his own daughter who wants him to do it. Quite right, too."

I was getting heartily sick of Herman Miller's daughter, her adorable children, and both of her husbands. The prospect of discussing the ex-husband's new wife didn't enthrall me at all, and I was overfull of tea. I managed to hitch my butt far enough forward to deposit the porcelain that still encumbered my knees on the tray that sat on the coffee table, hoping Karen would take the hint.

Instead, she sipped at the fresh tea Mrs. Eskew had poured for her and asked, very casually, "What was his first son-in-law's name?"

"Why, let me see." Mrs. Burnham posed with her index finger against her chin and her thumb supporting it. "Anderson, I believe. John Anderson?" She peered at me from under half-lowered lids. "Do you know, I'm not quite sure what his first name is. Isn't that odd? But he's called Bucky, that I do know."

She smiled pleasantly at me and lifted her cup to her lips while little bits of puzzle clicked into place in my mind.

XV

KAREN TWISTED THE key in the back-door lock and leaned it open. "I'm going to call Anderson's wife," she said. "Didn't you say he gave you the number?"

"He thought he was giving me his," I said.

"But you matched it with her address. He must just have forgotten and given you his old phone number under the stress of the moment."

"He didn't look very stressed," I remarked, opening the drawer under the telephone for the address book. "In fact, he was so cool I didn't even see how it could be the same guy I talked to the morning after Rogers was shot."

"We'll see." Karen had thumbed the red leather book open to the A's and already had the receiver in her hand, dialing. A moment later she slammed her free hand down on the hook and frowned at me. "A man answered," she said.

I shrugged. "Maybe she's got what Sarah Burnham would probably describe as a gentleman caller. She is separated from him, remember."

"Or maybe . . . there's another possibility." Karen sucked in her lips, frowning hard. "The phone book comes out in December, and they only separated last summer. What if he took the telephone number with him? And she got the new one?"

"Could happen, I guess."

"What was that address?"

I pointed to the red book still lying on the countertop and opened the refrigerator to investigate the possibility of a snack. "A Mrs. Anderson," I heard Karen say. She gave the address. "Yes, that's right. It would be a new listing."

I found a little bit of raspberry yogurt in the bottom of a container and leaned against the counter to eat it. Karen was

158

dialing again. She turned her back to me, as if she were embarrassed, and a few seconds later said, "Mrs. Anderson?"

The day's trash had already gone into the outside can. I got a brown paper bag out and opened it and stood it in the corner and threw the empty yogurt cup into it.

" . . . looking for a Mrs. Anderson who was—is—the daughter of Herman Miller of Fox Prairie, Minne—oh. . . . You wouldn't— Thanks very much," she snapped. "Sorry to bother you."

She hung up and faced me again, cheeks flushed. "Mrs. Anderson is not the daughter of any Herman Miller of any-where on earth," she said. "Her maiden name is Flagstad, thank-you-very-much. Mrs. Anderson doesn't know anything about the Miller woman and would people please quit bothering her about the bitch, she has other problems on her mind."

"That's that, I guess."

"Too bad." Karen sighed and sank into a chair by the kitchen table. "It looked like a good lead."

"Especially since our John Anderson would also have had the expertise to pull this particular joke on his boss."

"Right." Karen picked at a bit of dried tomato sauce on the glossy surface of the table. "But, come to think of it, why should he?"

I shrugged and sat down across from her. "You met Rogers. I bet he was damned hard to work for. You heard him on the phone to Anderson."

"I didn't, actually, but you told me about it. I agree, I wouldn't want to be treated like that. But he's the head technician, so he must have something on the ball, mustn't he?" She cocked her head at me. "Why not just switch jobs? Why stay and take that kind of nonsense for, what did Cam say, ten years?"

I glanced at the clock. Twenty to six. "Search me. And one other question, before I go haul Joey out of Gary's sandbox. Who else has been asking our Mrs. Anderson questions?"

"Jackson Powell, of course. Who else?" As I reached for the back-door knob, Karen added, "Joe, after all that tea and sweetness, I've got absolutely no ambition. What do you say we eat at Burger King tonight?"

*   *   *

Powell it had been. He was waiting in the blue van when we got back from Burger King, chortling over his new prize: the now Mrs. Anderson was a second wife, and the first just might have been named Emily Miller, though he wasn't sure. "See what that means, don't you?" he gloated, following Karen into the house.

Joey pulled at my sleeve. "Daddy, who is that man?" he whispered. "How come he keeps coming around?"

"He's just somebody Mommy and I met while we were on our trip," I explained, sotto voce. "Nobody to worry about. And it's time for you to be getting ready for bed, young man—it's late, and there's school tomorrow."

"Aw, Dad!"

"Now."

Once again, Karen was fitting a filter into the coffeepot and Powell was sitting spread-kneed at our kitchen table with one fist clasped in the other hand. "I can't prove it yet," he said. "I have to wait for the state offices to open tomorrow. But I know in my bones that first wife was Herman Miller's daughter."

"Why don't you just call Herm and ask?" Karen asked.

"Are you kidding? After that story in the newspaper everybody from five states around has been tramping over his field this weekend, taking souvenirs of the dirt. He's lost two yards of topsoil by the tablespoonful. He'd take his shotgun to me if he could, you betcha."

"I'll call him, then," Karen said.

"You want him to tip Anderson off?" Powell demanded. "You don't think anybody messed around in that field without Miller in on it, do you?"

"Miller was away," I said.

"He says."

"At a stock auction. He bought a cow for his grandson, so he could probably prove it," Karen pointed out.

Powell said, "Ahh!" in the soft crow of a man who sees all in a flash. "That's interesting. That's very interesting."

"Why?"

"I figure it went something like this," Powell explained. "Anderson knew Miller would be gone, buying a cow for his

160

son, so he went down there Saturday afternoon and set the thing up, using a hunting trip as a cover story. Then, Saturday night he went back and did the red-light routine, using a police-band radio to warn him if any deputies were coming. What the flash of light was, I don't know yet, but it shouldn't have been too hard to rig something. When he figured he'd done enough, he got out of there on his motorbike. Good?"

"Could be," I said.

"How could he carry all that stuff on a motorbike?" Karen asked. "And do you even know he has one?"

"He'd only need to carry the red light and the flasher," Powell said. "He's got an 'eighty-three Dodge Sportsman that'd hold everything else *and* the bike—that's a Yamaha. No problem there."

Joey, in pajamas, peered around the edge of the kitchen door. "Have you brushed your teeth and washed up?" Karen asked.

He nodded solemnly and said, "I want Daddy to tuck me in tonight."

"Hold on a minute," I replied.

"No, that's okay, this can wait a few minutes." Powell said. "Tuck the kid in, then we can talk this over. 'Night, Joey."

Joey squeezed out a polite answer and took my hand and tugged me across the family room and into the short hall that leads to the bathroom and bedrooms. His own room had a small-boy smell compounded of leather and candy wrappers and autumn leaves. I crossed to the window and pushed it shut the remaining two inches. "Supposed to get colder tonight," I said.

"Lock it, Daddy." Joey bounced onto his bed, round-eyed and skinny and slightly pale.

"Lock it? What's the matter?"

"That man," he whispered. "I saw him walking around last night and he scares me."

"Walking around?" I sat on the bed beside him and stared into his face. "What do you mean?"

"Out the side window," he whispered. "See? You can see the street in front of Mrs. Eskew's house. He left his van there and got out and walked down the sidewalk and walked back up and he sitted there a long, long time."

"When was that?"

"In the middle of the night. I heared you snoring, Dad. And the lights were all out. I had to go to the bathroom," he added quickly, as if he thought he'd just gotten himself in hot water. "That's how come I was awake. And when I came back to bed the moon was shining and I looked out the window before I got under the covers. That's when I seed him. Then I couldn't sleep and I was thinking, what if he's still there? So I looked again, and that van *was* still there."

I reached out and pushed the hair back off his forehead. "Why didn't you tell me before?" I asked.

Joey hugged his knees and rested his chin on them. "I didn't know you'd let him in the house again," he said. "Did he do something bad?"

"I don't think so."

"He's not a kidnapper, is he?"

Fighting an odd sensation of something lurching at the base of my brain, I said, "No, he's not a kidnapper," hoping with a blend of disbelief and amusement that would reassure my son. I've never been quite certain how much he remembers about the time he really was kidnapped, before he was two. "It's okay, so don't you worry," I said. I smiled. "Scrunch yourself down under those blankets and I'll tuck you in."

He did, and I did. I stopped at the door and looked back at him before I turned off the light. Nothing showed but the top of his head above his ears. The one eye I could see was squeezed shut. I said, "Good night, small Joseph," an old ritual we hadn't used in months.

"Good night, big Joseph," he murmured sleepily. I left the door standing ajar and went back to the kitchen.

"Promise me, the minute you get any kind of information, you'll call me," Powell was saying to Karen as she poured out the coffee. "I want this tied down just as tight as I can get it. Then we can go confront the guy and he'll probably be delighted to explain exactly how he did it."

"Another story?" I asked.

Powell grinned. "Why not? That's how I make my living."

I sat down. An image of Herman Miller walking across his field in the dark flickered at the back of my mind. For once, I paid attention to this subconscious warning; Miller had said, *It's my land, isn't it?* And if it had been a UFO at the bottom of that field? Miller could have been in deep trouble defending his territory. As I might be if I confronted Powell about parking his van near my house in the middle of the night. if Karen's suspicion of the man was accurate. Then, too, it was possible Joey had been mistaken. . . . A lot of people own vans. . . .

"I've got a question for you," I put into the conversation a couple of minutes later. "You read those interview transcripts. Remember that one of those kids shined a light where she thought the red light had come from? And she didn't see anybody."

"I'm not impressed." Powell stopped to swallow some coffee. "Oh, that's good! Anderson was a Green Beret. He'd know how to camouflage himself for a situation like that."

"What about his red beach ball?" Karen asked.

"Who knows?" Powell asked, a little irritably. "Maybe he sat on the damn thing." He stared at the table and sipped a little more coffee. "The only thing left is the radioactivity. It keeps coming back to the radioactivity. I'm damned if I can figure that. Almost makes me believe in the thing."

I glanced up at Karen, who shook her head slightly. So I kept quiet, though Powell was probably the one who could find out who was missing a dollop of iron-59 if anyone could. And Karen could well be right: what possible reason for following us around could Powell have, what reason for staking out our house, except to see how close we were to catching up with him? What a story that hoax would make . . . and Powell had left out much of his interview with me last summer. Who knows what he had left out that Rogers had told him?

That thought made me doubly glad I hadn't confronted him with Joey's story.

Monday was a normal day, to begin with. I got in at seven-thirty as usual, sat down with some of my engineers to map out the week's work as usual, ate out of the vending machines as usual.

But Monday is our letter carrier's day off, and the sub walks the route in the opposite direction, so it was only eleven-thirty when the mail came to the house, and Karen called me. "You got a letter," she said. "The return address just says 'Angie,' but it's marked *Important.* Do you want me to open it and read it to you?"

"Sure, go ahead."

I heard the envelope tear and the sheet of paper crackle as Karen opened it out. "Oh, my goodness," she said. "She says, 'I'm the lab tech who was in the lab when you talked to Bucky Anderson.' Does that make sense?"

"Yes, go on." Angie: I remembered Anderson's dry response to the girl.

" 'You should know Bucky does all the ordering around here. Cam just signed the sheets without even looking. Bucky does everything, in fact. I don't know if Cam even thought about anything but laying every female in sight. Even me—he wasn't prejudiced. Every once in a while Bucky would bring Cam up to date so he'd know what he was talking about when he had to say something about his research,' " Karen read. "*His* is in quotes."

"Cute."

"Wait, she goes on," Karen said. " 'Bucky even ordered isotopes on Cam's license. He could put in for anything he damn pleases, maybe plutonium even.' "

"That's probably an exaggeration."

"Sure it is. You want to hear the rest of this or not?"

"Go on."

" 'Bucky hated Cam. I don't know why he kept working for him except maybe it's the only way he'd get to run a lab without a degree. He's a lot smarter than Cam was, but he let Cam use his brain. What a wimp! So I bet it was Bucky pulled that joke about the UFO. It's the kind of thing he'd laugh about the rest of his life and never let on. Every time Cam started acting that superior, Bucky would be thinking screw you.' " I heard the paper crackle again. "It's signed *Angie B.*"

164

"Well, there we are," I said. "Looks like Powell's right, after all. Anderson had his little joke."

"He went to a lot of trouble for it."

"I've ceased to be amazed at convoluted minds," I said. "I've worked for too many. I wonder what he thought of the consequences, though?"

"Why don't you ask him?"

Sarcasm. "Come on, Karen, you know I can't do that. I would like to get the thing tidied up completely, though. Prunella won't be happy until all the loose ends are tied up in bows. You know how she is about CATCH's reputation."

Karen sighed, a blast into the telephone. "Well, I don't know what you expect to do. You can hardly get a search warrant."

"Hey, wait," I said. "That's an idea. There's an apartment in Anderson's building for rent—want to go look at it with me?"

"Are you nuts, Joe?"

"No, really. Remember that place we lived in on Dupont? That storage area in the basement? Anderson's building is just like that, on the outside anyway, so I bet we could get a look into his. S'pose I take a couple of hours off and we go find out."

Karen said nothing for about thirty seconds. I was about to resign the idea when she said, "Well, I've gone along this far, I may as well finish it out. I'll see if Gary's mother will let the boys play over there while I'm gone."

"Karen," I said urgently. "Don't forget to make sure you don't see Powell's van around anywhere before you come out, okay?"

Neither the liver and white dog nor the woman with the tired shopping bags was in sight. Otherwise, the building was just as I remembered it, down to the peeling sign for the two-bedroom apartment. Karen parked the station wagon and examined the place from across the street. "I'll tell you, Joe, now that I'm no longer a starving student you couldn't pay me to live in that place," she said.

"I'm not asking you to sign a lease, for God's sake," I pointed out. "Come on, let's go."

I looked again at the building. Metal-framed windows, rot-free in Florida, that here would be furry with frost all winter.

Brick losing its mortar from the uncapped sills beneath them. Cheap fifties construction, like a hundred thousand other buildings just like it all over the United States. A little green car coming down the street ducked into a parking space before it got to us, and we crossed.

A gray metal door with one vertical slot of a window opened directly into the stairwell. *Inquire at Apt. 1-B,* the sign said. Beside a door next to the stairs another, smaller sign identified one of two apartments as 1-B, the occupant as the building manager. A television blared behind 1-B's gray metal door, a door rusting around the edges, featureless except for the pustule of a viewing lens. Karen flicked me a disgusted glance and pushed the bell beneath the number.

A narrow, collapsed face topped by red hair in brush curlers edged around the door as it opened the hand's-breadth the chain would allow. "What do you want?" the woman asked. I could see a slice of pink chenille bathrobe even though it was early afternoon, and the voices of the tormented actors in the room behind her echoed in the stairwell.

"We were driving past when we saw the sign for the apartment," I said. "Is it still available?"

"Oh." The woman looked at Karen, then back at me. "Yeah, it's available," she said. "Hold on." The door shut in our faces and the deadbolt turned audibly.

"Getting dressed," Karen remarked.

I leaned against the wall and looked out the narrow, wire-meshed window at our car across the street, neatly framed from hood ornament to back bumper between the edges of the glass. Paint was curling off the inside of the outer door, and the stairwell foyer smelled strongly of damp concrete, rust, and Lysol. The door behind me clicked. As I turned, I caught sight of someone passing the building out of the tail of my eye, a plumpish man with a hat pulled low over his near ear. Before I could step to the door to see if it really had been Jackson Powell or if I had begun having paranoid hallucinations, the red-haired woman came out of her apartment and locked the door behind her. "Velma Murdoch," she announced. "And you?"

"Karen and Joe Jamison," Karen said, before I could get in with my made-up name.

Ms. Murdoch was wearing jeans and fuzzy blue slippers and a blue sweatshirt that said, *Well, it ain't as boring as that alligator* across the chest. "Two-B," she tossed over her shoulder, walking between me and the front door to get to the stairs. She started to climb without looking back, sorting through a bunch of keys. Karen took a deep breath and climbed after her. I got a quick look out the door window as I went by, saw nobody, saw no blue van.

Two-B was, in a word, depressing. Karen proved herself a trooper. She examined the one closet, paced off the dimensions of the rooms without having to exert herself very much, flushed the toilet and watched it gurgle, turned on the water in the kitchen and reduced it to its former drip, just as if she might take the apartment. "No refrigerator?" she asked.

"Nah, that you got to get your own, Mrs. Jamison."

"What about getting the stove cleaned?" Karen asked, bending down to look into a crusted oven.

"Oh, sure, Mrs. Jamison, that'll be taken care of," the Murdoch woman said easily. By the next tenant.

"And the holes in the wall in the living room?"

"Sure, Mrs. Jamison, we'll plaster them over before you move in." The woman was thawing now, surer of her prospects. Her hands rested on her hips, fingers uncrossed. The nails of her left hand had been polished a deep maroon; those on her right hand were cracked and yellowed, bare of polish. "Paint the place, too, Mrs. Jamison, any color you want so long as it's white."

"White's fine."

The "Mrs. Jamison" business was getting on my nerves. Somebody must have told the woman that you get a better reception by repeating a prospect's name; I've noticed that other salespeople do it, too. It echoed unpleasantly in the bare rooms, as did the muffled television from downstairs.

Karen turned in a small circle in the middle of the living room. "It's a little small," she said doubtfully.

"So's the rent, Mrs. Jamison."

Karen went back into the kitchen and opened one of the cupboards. Something scurried away from the light. She shuddered. "What about the bugs?" she asked.

"Oh, yeah, we'll have the exterminator in, Mrs. Jamison," the manager promised cheerfully. "I can see you're a clean-living woman, Mrs. Jamison. That's the kind of tenant we like."

"Is there more storage room?" I asked.

"Sure." Velma Murdoch was almost expansive now. "There's a big locker in the basement."

"Could we see it?"

"Sure thing, Mr. Jamison." She went through the apartment, snapping off lights, and opened the door.

"What about pets?" I asked.

"We don't like pets, Mr. Jamison, I'll be honest with you, but there's nothing in the lease against them. Two-A has a dog."

"Does it make much noise?"

"Not usually. It's a hunting dog, I guess Bucky's got it trained pretty good." The woman tried the door of 2-B to be sure it had locked, and started down the stairs. "No, sir, Mr. Jamison, that dog shouldn't bother you at all," she called back at me. Karen started down the stairs behind her. Behind the door of 2-A I heard the same questioning "Whuf?" I'd heard two days before, then silence.

The basement door, more leprous gray steel, was tucked under the angle of the stairs. Ms. Murdoch unlocked it with one of the keys on the big ring. "We keep this locked at all times," she said. "You'd have your own key, naturally. Mr. Jamison." "At all times" seemed to be an exaggeration; she expertly kicked a worn wooden wedge under the bottom edge of the door to hold it open and started down a dim set of stairs.

Two unshaded forty-watt bulbs lit the basement, one in the middle of the ceiling and the other over a coin-op washer and dryer. "You don't want to spend the day down here, Mrs. Jamison, there's a Laundromat just down the block," Ms. Murdoch said. "It ain't any cleaner, but it's brighter, and there's people to talk to."

Brighter: a good point. The two bulbs hardly supplemented the blue wash of light from the four small windows masked by

168

shrubs. None of it made it as far as a corner. A dark, square furnace squatted in the corner near the washing machine. Nearby, three dusty blue-and-white water heaters hissed quietly. The pilot lights reflected blue on the floor beneath them.

"I gen'ly bring a flashlight down," Ms. Murdoch said. "There ain't any lights in the bins. Yours is empty, though, you won't have any trouble seeing how big it is. Mrs. Jamison."

Karen glanced at me, lips tight and the tip of her tongue just showing between them; she'd seen what I'd seen, that the "bins" were made of chainlink fence, and that 2-B's shared a "wall" with 2-A's.

"You wouldn't want to put anything real valuable down here, Mr. Jamison," the manager said. She padded across the floor toward the six enclosures lined up on a long wall and lifted the hasp of 2-B's bin. "You have to supply your own padlock, naturally. 'Course, you could put something up inside the chainlink so's nobody could see in, then maybe you could store something a little more stealable, but I don't think it's a good idea."

"Bad neighborhood?" Karen asked.

"Not as bad as some," the manager said. "We ain't had any murders around here. Couple rapes is all."

Karen said, "Oh."

"Break-ins, that's another story, see," Ms. Murdoch continued with aplomb. "And down here, you wouldn't likely get interrupted if you wanted to clean out a bin."

"I see." Karen had ventured into the bin belonging to 2-B. One of the four inadequate windows, being centered on the wall, was divided between it and the bin next to it. I heard her take a shaky breath. "Oh, I see what you mean," she said. "Anybody could see what there was to take." She gestured toward the adjoining bin. "See, Joe?"

I saw. Behind a normal agglomeration of footlocker, cartons, and bundles, I saw a large parabolic reflector with a net stretched over the back of it. Bits of leaf and grass still clung to the net. A wire, not attached to anything now but with its alligator clips dangling free, had been snaked under the open fabric and out at the edge. All you'd need to do to hide the whole thing would be to set the reflector down over any gear you had, like a battery . . . good enough while the man you'd just blinded with a flash stumbled away and you hid in the brush with your own camouflage. A reflector that size would even cover a flashlight and a red plastic ball. Very neat.

Standing against the back wall next to the reflector was a pair of snowshoes, the oval, tailless kind, padded with old blankets and heavy plastic. "Yeah, you're right," I said. The last bits of the hoax, falling nicely into place.

"I think we've seen enough," Karen said brightly as she turned toward Velma Murchison. Her mouth dropped into an O and her eyes widened.

The building manager and I turned in unison to see what Karen was staring at.

"Maybe you've seen too much," Anderson said. He stood halfway down the basement stairs with a gun, a handgun this time, in his good left fist.

XVI

ANDERSON CAME DOWN two more steps, his shoulder against the concrete block wall beside him. "How did you get onto it, Jamison?" he asked.

"Process of elimination."

"Don't give me that. That sheriff is still farting around with those jerk-offs in Fox Prairie, and I can guarantee you're no smarter than he is."

"Somebody told—"

"Karen!"

She glanced at me and shut up.

"Angie, I'll bet," Anderson said. Neither of us moved. The gun waved slightly to our left. "Come on, Velma, get back in the group," he said. "Must have been Angie," he said to me. "She's the only one who knew we had talked about it."

The building manager had sidled back to us and was busy working her way around behind me. "What in God's name is this all about, Bucky?" she asked.

Anderson ignored the question. "What'd she do—call you? Write to you? Funny. I should have thought of that. She takes such rotten lab notes, I never thought of a letter." He sighed. "I suppose she got your address off Cam's desk. Too bad. I missed the first chop—out of practice, after nearly twenty years. It got pretty bloody."

"You killed somebody?" Velma Murdoch squealed.

"You mean Jamison didn't tell you that? It was on the TV news yesterday. It's all over the paper this morning. Where she worked, even. When I saw that, I knew it was only a matter of time before you came looking for proof, but I only beat you here by five minutes." He shook his head. "Comes of being too responsible. I didn't get to the paper until lunch."

I hadn't looked at that morning's paper myself, beyond a

glance at the headlines and the comics, but now I remembered the name from the news the night before. Tabitha A. Brent. Angie B. No wonder I hadn't made the connection. "Over a hoax, Anderson?" I asked incredulously. "What did you do that was even illegal? Besides spreading a little radioactivity around."

He laughed. "Are you trying to make me believe you don't know I shot Cam? Come off it, Jamison—I'd try to save my skin too, but that's ridiculous. Give me credit for more brains than that."

"Oh, yes," I said, stalling. "Angie did say you were the brains behind Rogers's research." Stalling for what? The stairs were the one way out. If I could persuade him to lock us into the bin, maybe, while he got away?

"That bastard took everything I had," Anderson said. "My work, my degree, both my wives—" He broke off. "No, no. No distractions."

Rogers was the "dago" Anderson's first wife ran off with! His dark eyes, glossy brown hair—

Anderson said, "You should have kept your wife out of this, Jamison. Don't you care what happens to her? I cared what happened to mine."

"Of course I—"

"Shut up. I'm trying to decide if I'd have enough time if I just locked you up. What time is it, half-past one?"

The light behind Anderson brightened slightly. The silhouette of half a head slowly materialized at the edge of the doorway at the top of the stairs, then withdrew. A moment or two later it reappeared, followed by the rest of the policeman inching silently down the stairs, left hand just touching the wall behind him, right hand clutching a gun.

Anderson must have heard something I didn't—a breath, or the scrape of the bullet-proof vest against the concrete. He whirled and fired. An answering shot spat down the stairs and stung chips and sparks from the concrete floor. "Take cover down there," boomed a voice.

"Over here!" Velma Murdoch dived for the squat bulk of the furnace. Anderson sent a shot after her; sparks flew from the wall. My head was ringing.

The cop hurtled down the steps against Anderson's side. He got off another shot, wild, that sent splinters flying from the joists over our heads. Karen rolled behind the furnace to crouch with the building manager. Room only for two: I sprinted for the water heaters only to find that the space between them and the wall wouldn't have held a cat.

One of the shots had nicked a gas pipe. The odors of the gunshots and of the garlic they put in gas made me choke. "The pilots," Velma Murchison screamed.

More blue uniforms hustled down the stairs and joined the struggle where Anderson had now fallen to the floor. I crawled along the line of water heaters, wrenching off the coverplates and turning the red knobs beneath them to *Off*. "Drop it," someone demanded between clenched teeth. "Drop it, drop it, drop it."

"Look out!" Another shot, and the crash of glass as a window went out. Velma Murdoch slipped along the wall toward the gas meter and turned the brass valve. The hissing I'd barely heard stopped. A gun came spinning across the floor and clanged against the skirt of one of the water heaters.

"Got him," said one of the cops, with satisfaction. "Get some cuffs on him."

Anderson was dragged to his feet and pushed up the stairs. One of the cops took Karen by the elbow and peered into her face. "You all right?" he asked. I saw her nod, and started across the cellar toward her, but my knees gave way. The pain as my kneecaps hit the floor drove everything else out of my mind.

XVII

"IF YOU HAD even just told me about the damn dog," Jackson Powell said. He tipped his weight onto fingers splayed on my kitchen table and stared at me. "Don't you know a pointer when you see one?"

"Sorry. I don't know much about dogs."

Karen reached into the cupboard next to the stove for some coffee mugs and Powell thumped into his chair. This was getting to be a regular routine. "A pointer is a hunting dog, J.J.," Powell said, half-strangled with patience. "And it howled all night the night Anderson was supposed to be out hunting—the night of the saucer hoax. I ask you, what grouse hunter leaves his bird dog home?" He nodded at Karen as she started to pour into the line of three mugs out of a milk carton. "Thanks," he said, reaching for the first of the mugs. "For that matter, there's a lot I don't understand," he complained. "Like, how did you get onto Anderson?"

I accepted a mug from Karen and put it down in front of me on the table. "First, he was the one who'd know how to cut up that rabbit—"

"Christ, J.J., anybody can gut a rabbit."

"Yes, but Anderson did it the way it was done in his lab."

"Sort of as a warning to Rogers, I think," Karen put in. "So he could tell himself afterward that he'd played fair, given Rogers enough time to save himself."

Powell screwed up his plump little mouth and waited.

"Second, he's the only one with access to radioactive material—and he even told me exactly how he used it. Not that I realized what he was doing."

"More rabbit," Karen suggested.

"Or something else to laugh about in the shower."

"As a matter of fact, he wasn't the only one with access to

174

radioactive materials," Powell said. "The high school has been designated for a special program in physics where the *kids* get to use it. It's kept locked up, but you know kids."

"Was it iron that they used?"

Powell shrugged. "That I don't know. Ed Gustafson might have been able to get something from one of his friends; I think he knows everybody in the county. The only one that lets out is Miller, when you get down to it."

"Third, the letter from the technician. I wish she'd signed her whole name, but I guess she was afraid to or something. If she had, I'd have realized who she was, and I'd have known Anderson was dangerous. Right up to the last minute, I was looking for a hoaxer, not a murderer."

"What do you mean, her whole name?"

"She's the girl who was killed last weekend. The one in the alley, in Dinkytown? She signed herself 'Angie B.' How the hell was I to know her first name was Tabitha?" The letter itself had been handed over to the police as evidence, but Karen had made a photocopy first. She passed it across the table to Powell.

"Hell, and this didn't tell you Anderson killed Rogers?"

Anger flared briefly: at Powell, for my own stupidity. "I was still thinking of an elaborate joke, and she doesn't say anything there that sounds as if the guy's murderous—just a practical joker. And I thought the sheriff was right, that the two incidents weren't really connected."

"I wish you'd told me about the radioactive iron when you found out," Powell said wistfully. "I thought we were working together."

Karen said, "We thought you might be the killer, keeping tabs on us."

"Me?"

"Because of that bull about the rifle."

Powell's thin fair skin flushed. "Oh, that." He sipped at his coffee. "How did you know?"

"You knew too much else about living in the country not to know that birds aren't hunted with rifles."

"Oh." Powell stared out the kitchen window for a moment.

"See, that's the story I told the sheriff. So I figured I'd better tell you the same one, in case you ever compared notes. I didn't think I ought to tell him I'd brought the gun down with me on purpose, not when I'd met Rogers before."

"On purpose?" Karen asked. "For what?"

"Well." He sighed. "I thought I could get the saucer story wrapped up in half the time my editor thought it might take, and get a few hours of hunting in. I had in mind a rabbit, believe it or not. And it doesn't look good to say you've planned to play hookey, not when it's sure to get back to your boss."

"You seemed surprised to hear the gun was loaded," Karen remarked.

"Jesus, was I! I don't know where my head was last week. I'm not generally that careless. Here I'd been riding around with the van unlocked half the time, some kid could've—well." He closed his eyes and sighed again. "Nobody did, thank the good Lord."

"Speaking of the van. How come you were following us around?"

"Keeping an eye on you, J.J., as much as I could." Powell's grin turned down at the corners. "I was working on a story, you know. Rogers's murder. I thought you might lead me to the killer if I let you putz around with that hoax business long enough."

"In the middle of the night?"

"I don't get you."

"You scared my son half to death. He saw you park in front of my neighbor's house and come down toward our house in the middle of the night. He thought you might kidnap him."

"Kidnap!" Powell's mouth closed with a pop. "Never. That wasn't the middle of the night anyway, it wasn't even midnight. I was going to check something out with you, but the house was dark so I went back to my van and figured it out myself. You guys go to bed at the crack of twilight, that's your trouble."

"You could have told me what you were up to."

"How did I know for sure you hadn't shot the guy yourself?"

My turn to gape. Outside, the wind began to rise, slapping a wet snow against the dark window glass. The furnace fan came

176

on. "Oh, come on," Powell said over the domestic noises. "You and Karen were the only witnesses. You could have stashed a rifle across the road, left a little after Rogers, sprinted to get ahead of him, and shot him. Ditch the rifle and tell your story and you're home free."

"I was wounded myself." I scratched at my arm, from which the scab had started to peel. "Just a burn, but I wouldn't let anybody take a shot at me. Not even Karen."

"Maybe especially Karen!" Karen exclaimed with horror. "I've never fired a gun in my life!"

"You were shot? I didn't know that."

I rolled my sleeve up and showed Powell the bright line of shiny new skin across my upper arm. He whistled through his teeth. "Close."

"Too close." I rolled the sleeve back down and buttoned the cuff. "Like Monday afternoon. How come you happened along just then?"

"Like before. I was tailing you, looking for my story."

"I didn't see your van."

"I had my sister's Datsun." *The little green car.* "Only I didn't know why you went to that building. I trailed you there Saturday, of course—"

"What about the guy with the chain saw?" I asked.

"Oh, him. That was a couple of weeks ago, really, but it was handy."

Guile layered upon guile. "What about the kids you took to Como Park Zoo?" I asked. "Are they figments, too?"

Powell's face sobered. "They're real," he said shortly. "About Monday. I was actually in the building when Anderson went after you. I'd gone in and heard you talking in the basement—Jeez, that woman has a loud voice—and I decided to look at nameplates to see who you were interested in. I knew damn well you weren't looking to rent a roach trap like that! I was just reading Anderson's card when the dog whined and I heard steps coming to his door. I hotfooted it up to the third-floor landing to get out of his way, and when I saw the gun in his hand, I followed him down the stairs in my sock feet and ran like blazes down to the Laundromat to call the cops."

"So you didn't hear why he did it."

"Not out of his own mouth, no. But I heard that Anderson's first wife, Herm Miller's daughter, left him and ran off with Rogers. It didn't work out and she ended up marrying somebody else. A little later Anderson got married again too. That nice lady worked in another lab in the building, and Rogers went after her. Last summer somebody walked in on them making it on a pile of lab coats in front of the white rats. Can you see it?" Powell tittered. "So Anderson left her. And apparently what this letter says is true—it was an open secret that Anderson did all of Rogers's real work all this time. I guess it got to be too much, and Anderson set up his trap, which Rogers sprang."

"I can see why it might have been too much," I said. "More coffee?"

"Thanks." Powell watched the thick brown stream splash into his cup. "Anderson should have just let somebody else do the shooting," he said. "I guess he couldn't even trust Rogers to be bastard enough to tempt some other sucker into finishing him off. He'd have gotten clean away if he had."

"Didn't you once tell me you didn't have a devious mind?" Karen asked. Powell smiled.

Karen frowned. "What I don't understand is why," she said. "Why stay with Rogers all those years when he was being used like a . . . a piece of toilet paper? It doesn't make sense."

We sat staring at our empty mugs. The snow had changed to rain, a rattle against the kitchen window. The house creaked in a sudden gust. "Winter," Powell said. His voice was very soft.

"Maybe he was a drug addict," Karen burst out. "Some men came back addicted to heroin, didn't they? Maybe Rogers kept him supplied. . . . "

Powell was shaking his head. "No sign of that," he said. "Though, according to that nice lady in the sheriff's office—"

"Old Stoneface?" I asked, an octave above my usual pitch.

"That nice lady," Powell corrected. "You've just got to appreciate what a thankless job hers is sometimes. Buy her a little lunch, a cup of coffee. . . . Anyway, according to her, Rogers heard something about that cocaine deal that was going down

178

last weekend and tried to put a little muscle on somebody. They were working hard on that angle until Anderson confessed."

I stared at Karen, who was staring at me. "When the hell did he have time to do that?" I asked.

"We didn't hold his hand every minute," Karen murmured.

"No."

"Then I don't know," she said, reverting to Anderson. "Some kind of misplaced loyalty? Were they together in the army?"

"That's something I ought to check." Powell hauled his notebook out of his sagging jacket pocket and wrote himself a reminder.

"I'll tell you one thing," I said. "The guy's a good actor. That phone call, the morning after—I'd have staked my good right arm that he was shocked to hear that Rogers was dead. I guess he was just checking up on his marksmanship, but he sounded really shaken."

Karen said, "Maybe he was."

"I don't get you."

She looked toward the window, where the half-rain half-snow was sliding into a thin gray line against the night at the bottom of each pane of glass. "I think maybe his revenge was sweetest in the plotting—he must have spent a lot of time on it, polishing each detail. Maybe he was hoping he'd missed, so he could go on plotting. Not having that to think about anymore would be a letdown, don't you think?"

"Maybe." I shifted my feet to ease my still-painful knees. "But when I talked to him in the lab he came across as . . . oh, ordinary. An ordinary helpful guy. I'd have staked my arm on that, too." I started to sigh and shook my head instead.

"Good thing you didn't stake any arms," Powell remarked. "Well, I've got to be going. Thanks for the coffee."

"Anytime," I said. That's what being fully socialized will do for you.

When I had seen Powell out the door I dialed the Committee for Analysis of Tropospheric and Celestial Happenings in Boston to report that I hadn't caught one this time, either. Prunella Watson's dry old voice turned gleeful as that of a child with a new puppy when I told her I was about to report. The glee died

179

as I explained and explained, until everything had been explained away and nothing was left. Finally she said, very sadly, "You've never come up with one about which there was any doubt, have you, J.J.?"

"No, Prue. Not once I got a good look."

"Oh well." She sighed. "You do what you have to do, and that includes explaining it all away, I guess."

"I'm sorry."

"Sorry! Oh dear, no. Don't be sorry." The verve was back in her voice. "You're doing an excellent job, no need for sorry! But there is one thing I don't understand. Why did that man take such an elaborate revenge? Why not just move elsewhere, much earlier?"

"Anderson? I guess we'll never know." We chatted a little longer, and I hung up, oddly depressed and dissatisfied with my beautiful case.

"We'll never know," Karen repeated. "Odd, isn't it? After all that?"

XVIII

THE FIRST REAL snow had fallen, leaving Karen's purple chrysan-themums capped with little blobs of white, before I got the last of our storm windows in place. I was hanging the kitchen screen in the rack in the garage when a large shadow fell across it. "Busy, busy," Mack said.

"Hi! Come on in and have some coffee," I said, slapping my hands together in my leather work gloves. "I'm frozen. Awful slop, isn't this?"

"Guy I work with says it's just like they have all winter long, back east. Can you imagine living with it that long?" Mack stomped the slush off his boots and followed me into the kitchen. He said, "I've got a present for you."

"What?" Mack and I are buddies from before we were as old as Joey, but we don't exchange gifts.

"Something on that murder you got yourself tangled up in last month. Anderson?"

"I'll be glad to hear the last of it," I said. "What, do you know when it's coming to trial? We already talked to the grand jury."

"No such luck. And like as not it'll be continued when it does come up. Anderson's got himself one of those courtroom clowns could make you believe you hear with your nose and blow snot out your ears. You'll be lucky if you're off the hook before you're a grandfather."

I shook the coffeepot and decided what was left was worth reheating. "That's a present?"

"Not that. I brought you the motive. The real, honest-to-God, guaranteed, behind-the-scenes motive."

"You're kidding."

"For that, you could make fresh coffee," Mack suggested pointedly. I slopped the contents of the pot into the sink and ran some cold water into it to rinse it.

"Okay?"

"Fine." Mack plopped into one of the kitchen chairs, which are sturdier than they look. "Professor of mine used to say, when you've got a crime you can't explain, look for the previous crime."

I thought about that for a second or two between scoops of coffee. "Some kind of blackmail?"

"I knew if I hung around long enough I'd find out why people always said you're so smart," Mack remarked. Unnecessarily, I thought. "Blackmail, yes, but no money involved. Anderson and Rogers were in high school together. They signed up and served in Vietnam in the same unit. And while they were there, Anderson killed a lieutenant. One of ours."

I lost count of the coffee measures. "Good God! And he wasn't caught?"

"You got to remember, J.J., Anderson's a brain. Like you."

"Thanks."

"He did it at night, planned for no witnesses. I guess the guy was making life in general miserable, and he wasn't the best at keeping his men and morale together. Anderson fixed it so it would look like the guerillas got him. Bayonneted the poor SOB, crushed his voicebox with his rifle butt, and left him to die with his guts hanging out. Only somehow, I don't know how, Rogers knew about it."

"I'd have kept my fat mouth shut if I were Rogers," I observed.

"Rogers wasn't you. He waited. He had a use for Anderson. Put a gun to his head and got him to write out a confession, which he squirreled away somewhere and used for leverage when the time came."

"That's nerve."

"Isn't that coffee done yet? Nerve, yes, but it worked. Rogers had some arrangement where if anything happened, et cetera, the letter would be opened, et cetera. You know the kind of deal."

"And that kept Anderson at heel?"

"Check. That was his life, in that envelope, check?" I poured out some of the coffee, kind of pallid still, but hot, and Mack took the cup.

"What changed?"

"Last summer, just about the time Rogers was breaking up Anderson's second marriage, the lawyer died. A whole box of stuff Rogers had left with him came to the lab and Rogers took it home. That night Anderson broke into Rogers's apartment and stole a bunch of stuff, including the box, and, as he'd hoped, the confession was there in the letter Rogers had been holding over his head. The original confession, check? Now, Anderson couldn't say anything to Rogers, or Rogers would have had him on the burglary. Besides, Anderson was after something a little more permanent. So he planned his trap, thinking he was clear."

"But," I supplied for him, so he could swallow some coffee.

Mack made a face. "Jeez, J.J., what is this swill? Where's your wife?"

"Grocery shopping."

"Gawd. My luck."

"But," I insisted.

"But he forgot the humble Xerox copier." Mack got up to examine the mysteries of the coffeepot. "It will all come out at the trial, of course, but I thought you'd like to hear before your beard turned gray."

"Thanks," I said, meaning it. I don't like loose ends.

Mack grinned. "I told you I'd brought you a present. Now, do yourself a favor and stick to your own job, check?"

"No more UFOs? You're as bad as Karen."

"Oh, them." Mack dismissed all such phenomena with a wave of one big hand. "No, I mean the coffee. See, you should have let it perk a little longer, that's all. Then maybe it would have tasted halfway decent, check?"

If you have enjoyed this book and would like to receive details of other Walker mystery titles, please write to:

Mystery Editor
Walker and Company
720 Fifth Avenue
New York, NY 10019